COMING HOME

BOOK 3 CRYSTAL LAKE SERIES

LAURA SCOTT

READSCAPE PUBLISHING, LLC

BOOKS BY LAURA SCOTT

Crystal Lake Series (listed in order)

Healing Her Heart

A Soldier's Promise

Coming Home

Worth The Wait

Christmas Reunion

Love Inspired Suspense Books

The Thanksgiving Target

Secret Agent Father

The Christmas Rescue

Lawman-In-Charge

Proof Of Life

Identity Crisis*

Twin Peril*

Undercover Cowboy*

Her Mistletoe Protector*

Wrongly Accused (SWAT Series)

Down To The Wire (SWAT Series)

Under The Lawman's Protection (SWAT Series)

Forgotten Memories (SWAT Series)

Holiday On The Run (SWAT Series)

Mirror Image (SWAT Series)

Shielding His Christmas Witness (Callahan Confidential)

The Only Witness (Callahan Confidential)

Christmas Amnesia (Callahan Confidential)

Shattered Lullaby (Callahan Confidential)

Primary Suspect (Callahan Confidential)

*Stories with Linked Characters

COMING HOME

By Laura Scott
Book 3 in the Crystal Lake Series

Cover art by The Killion Group, Inc.
Digital Formatting by Author E.M.S.

Please Note

This is a work of fiction. Names, characters, places and incidents are either the product of the author's imagination or are used fictitiously, and any resemblance to any actual persons living or dead, business establishments, events or locales is entirely coincidental.

Thank You

1

"Merry, I'm so glad you're here!" Janelle greeted her with a dramatic sigh as Merry entered the arena of the Hope County Hospital's Emergency Room. "I've been waiting forever for you to get here."

ER Charge Nurse Meredith Haines frowned at her nursing colleague. "What's the problem? I'm not late. I'm fifteen minutes early for my shift."

"I know, but look." Janelle jabbed her finger at the large whiteboard listing all the names of the current patients in the ER. "Leonard Marks is in room ten. He's been asking for you for the past five minutes. I've been trying really hard to keep him calm until you could get here."

Merry rolled her eyes. Janelle acted as if no one else was capable of taking care of Leonard. Sure, he was a mammoth of a man with a volatile psych history, but he'd been coming to the Hope County Hospital for his medical care long before she'd moved to Crystal Lake, a little over two years ago. Surely other nurses had taken care of him before?

"Okay, I'll go and see him," Merry said. "But I'm

supposed to be in charge, so I'll need you to make out assignments while I'm talking to Leonard."

"Thanks," Janelle said with a sigh of relief, tucking a dark strand of hair behind her ear. "Don't worry, I'll take care of the assignments. Anything to help you out. I don't know how you manage to deal so well with Leonard. Honestly? The guy scares me to death."

Merry's smile was a bit forced as she walked toward Leonard's room. She wasn't about to explain that she'd had lots of practice dealing with angry, psychotic men because she'd learned from firsthand experience.

She hadn't known about her former boyfriend's psych diagnosis until he'd attacked her.

The thought of Blake finding her sent a shiver down her spine. After leaving Minneapolis, she'd covered her tracks carefully. If Blake hadn't found her in more than two years, she didn't think he'd suddenly show up now.

Unfortunately, she knew far more about the complex world of psychiatric healthcare than she'd ever wanted to know. At least, today, she could put her knowledge and experience to good use.

Moving very slowly, to avoid any abrupt gestures, Merry carefully slid open the glass door to room ten and eased inside.

"Hi Leonard," she greeted him softly. "It's me, Merry."

"Merry! Where have you been?" Leonard demanded with the petulance of a small child, his gaze dark with reproach. "I've been waiting and waiting for you."

He was a full grown man of thirty-five, but his mind was that of a six-year-old. And often a bad tempered six-year-old, although she knew it wasn't his fault. Leonard had suffered a traumatic brain injury on top of his underlying schizophrenia, a combination that made him extremely difficult to manage.

Her stomach tightened when she didn't see any sign of Leonard's mother, Doreen. Had his mother dropped him off and then left? Normally, his mother stayed to help keep Leonard calm.

"I'm sorry, Leonard," she murmured, giving him a gentle smile. "But I'm here now. So tell me, what made you decide to come in to see us today?" Ironically, she'd learned Leonard didn't like the term *hospital* so she avoided using the reference if at all possible.

For a moment he looked truly bewildered. "I don't know." He rose to his feet and began to pace. "I have that feeling again. The one I don't like. The one that makes me mad. I hear voices telling me to do bad things."

Merry swallowed a knot of apprehension. The last few times Doreen brought Leonard to the ER, he'd complained of similar issues. Leonard was under a court order to take his psych meds, but his mother sometimes forgot. Merry was afraid Doreen Marks might be in the beginning stages of Alzheimer's disease. And if that was the case, Leonard would soon be too much for his mother to handle, if he wasn't already.

Without his medication, Leonard became lost in a sea of confusion. And when Leonard got confused, he got angry. And violent.

Leonard also had a medical history of poorly controlled diabetes and high blood pressure, but she couldn't even begin to examine him for his medical problems until she'd calmed him down.

"It's okay, Leonard," she said soothingly, placing a hand lightly on his arm. She was one of the few who could touch him without causing him to fly off in a rage. He tolerated women fairly well and, for once, her petite frame gave her an advantage. But Leonard didn't like men, especially those in uniform. When Leonard saw the police he went berserk, probably because he knew from several bad experiences that the arrival of the police meant he was taking a one-way trip to the mental health complex in Madison. "I'm here now. You know I'll take good care of you, right?"

"Right. Merry takes good care of me," he muttered as he pulled away from her and continued to pace. "Only Merry. No one else."

"All the nurses here take good care of you, Leonard. Not just me." She knew this odd dependence he had for her wasn't healthy. It wasn't as if she could possibly work every single day, all three shifts. "Don't worry, you're going to be fine."

The last time Leonard had come in, she'd succeeded in avoiding transferring him to the mental health facility. Once he'd taken meds to keep him calm, they'd evaluated his diabetes and his high blood pressure, making minor adjustments to his meds. By the end of the visit, he'd been able to go home with his mother, as docile as a bunny.

Maybe, just maybe, she'd be able to do that again. She wasn't sure who the doctor was on his team, but she needed to let him or her know that last time they'd started with a hefty dose of anti anxiety meds before getting him to take his usual dose of antipsychotic medication.

"Okay, Leonard, I want you to stay here. I'll be right

back. I'm going to get your favorite treat. Do you remember what your favorite treat is?"

Leonard was easily six feet tall and weighed two hundred eighty pounds, but a tremulous smile bloomed on his broad, square face. "Chocolate pudding!"

"That's right, chocolate pudding," she agreed with a smile. Sugar free chocolate pudding in deference to his diabetes, but he didn't need to know that. "Now be good and I'll get your treat, okay?"

Leonard nodded and she sent up a silent prayer on Leonard's behalf as she slid from his room. The poor man suffered more than anyone should have to. Grinding up pills and hiding the powder in the chocolate pudding was normally not an acceptable way to give patients their meds but, thankfully, Leonard's court order allowed them to do just that. During previous visits she'd been worried that he'd notice the slightly bitter taste but, every time, he'd gobbled up the pudding without detecting anything amiss.

Merry found Dr. Katy Albrecht hovering behind the desk, waiting for her. "I've ordered the Ativan for Leonard," Dr. Katy said before Merry could say anything. "The pharmacist is entering it in the system now."

"Thanks." Relieved that they were on the same page, Merry went over to the galley to grab two chocolate puddings from the tiny fridge. Then she stopped at the automated medication dispensing machine. It didn't take long to pull out the medications, crush the pills, and mix the powder in the pudding.

Satisfied, she shoved the spoon into the pudding and headed back across the arena to Leonard's room.

"Merry?" The sound of her name in a familiar, deep voice stopped her in her tracks. She braced herself before turning around to face police officer Zack Crain, who looked far too attractive in his dark blue uniform. He was tall, with short, dark hair and brilliant green eyes. Ever since she'd met Zack at his sister's wedding, her pulse jumped erratically when she was around him.

"Zack?" Her voice squeaked and she tried to get a grip. She licked her lips and tried again. "Hi. What are you doing here? I thought you worked in Madison?"

"I'm picking up the belongings from one of our car crash victims as potential evidence," he said. "Have you seen my sister, Julie? I was hoping to talk to her while I'm here."

"I'm sorry, but Julie and Derek are out of town enjoying a vacation alone while Lexi visits with her grandparents. I'm dog-sitting for them while they're gone." Merry glanced nervously over her shoulder towards Leonard's room. "Listen, Zack, I have a patient who doesn't like police, so please don't be upset, but I need to ask you to leave."

"Leave?" His eyebrows shot up in surprise, but then he scowled. "Don't worry, I'll be out of here as soon as security brings me what I need."

Merry didn't have time to argue. "Just wait someplace else, out of sight, okay?"

She turned back towards Leonard's room, but it was too late. Through the glass door, Leonard was staring in horror at Zack. There was a loud crash as Leonard slammed the bed up against the wall in a fit of anger.

"No cops!" he bellowed, lumbering out of his room, waving his arms wildly. "No cops!"

"Leonard, calm down. It's okay. I have your treat!" Merry planted herself directly in front of him, in a pathetic attempt to distract him from Zack, who she hoped and prayed was quickly ducking out of sight. "Look at me, Leonard." She captured his gaze with her own. "It's Merry, remember? I've promised to take good care of you. And I have your favorite treat!"

For a moment she thought she'd reached him, but then she saw Zack move up next to her as if he intended to protect her.

"No cops!" Leonard screamed. With a horrible keening wail, he brutally shoved Merry aside, sending her flying backward into the unforgiving corner of the nurse's station as he made a mad dash for the front door.

Oomph! She hit the edge of the counter, hard enough to steal the breath from her body, her left shoulder taking the brunt of the blow. She thought someone shouted her name over the din, but then a horrible pain exploded in her head.

Poor Leonard she thought, before darkness and pain closed around her.

ZACK STARED in horror when Merry flew into the side of the nurse's station. He heard her teeth snap together before she sailed backward, landing on the floor. Her head hit the linoleum with a sickening thud.

"Merry!" Zack was the first to reach her side, his heart thundering in his chest as he looked down at her pale, limp form. Most of the staff had gone to help bring the psychotic patient under control, and he knew he should have been helping, too, but he couldn't tear his gaze from Merry.

He forced himself to remember his basic medical training, but it wasn't easy. He gently lifted Merry's head to feel along the back of her scalp. His fingers came away wet. Stained red.

Blood. She was bleeding.

"Merry? Can you hear me?" He could barely hear himself, his heart was hammering so hard. "I'm here, and I won't leave you. Open your eyes, Merry. Can you talk to me?"

Nothing. She didn't move.

"I need some help over here," he called sharply, drawing a few stares from the group gathering around the patient who was still thrashing on the floor in spite of the pile of people trying to hold him down. He caught sight of a needle and syringe being plunged into the patient's thigh.

He couldn't suppress a flash of guilt, knowing that if he'd listened to Merry and left right away, this wouldn't have happened. But he hadn't understood the magnitude of danger. And when she faced the crazy man head on, he refused to leave her vulnerable and alone.

"Oh no, Merry!" A young female with deep red hair, wearing a long white lab coat, came to his aid. He figured she must be a doctor when she felt for Merry's pulse, and then pulled out a penlight to peer at her pupils.

"Can't we get her into a bed?" Zack asked. He didn't want to do anything that would hurt Merry, but he also didn't like seeing her stretched out on the floor.

Merry let out a soft moan and, despite her obvious pain, he was deeply relieved to know she was coming around.

"Try not to move." The female doctor's name tag identified her as Dr. Katy Albrecht. "We need to assess the extent of your injuries. Can someone get me a C-collar?" she called.

Given how hard her head had hit the floor, Zack assumed Merry had a concussion, but hopefully nothing worse. He assisted with lifting Merry's head just enough for Dr. Katy to get the cervical collar in place.

"Now we need a back board," Dr. Katy said, glancing up at the other staff members who huddled around Merry. "Which empty room can we use?"

"Room six is empty," a nurse by the name of Janelle said. "We can put Merry in there."

"Great, how's Leonard?" Dr. Katy asked in a distracted tone.

Zack assumed Leonard was the big man who'd gone crazy when he saw Zack's uniform. He glanced over the doctor's shoulder. The big man who'd been so crazy a few minutes ago was now being led back to his room by several of the staff the medications obviously working to calm him down. "He's fine from what I can tell," he told her.

"Here's the long board," Janelle said, hurrying over with a full-size plastic board with handles along the sides.

"We're going to roll Merry over on her side, and you're going to tuck the board underneath her, understand?" Dr. Katy addressed him as if he were one of her staff members.

He nodded, more than willing to help out if needed. "I have some basic first aid training, so I understand the concept of a log roll."

It took a few minutes to get Merry centered on the long board. Three other staff members helped him lift her up and carry her over to the empty room.

"My head hurts," Merry murmured, her face drawn with discomfort.

"Leonard knocked you down," Zack told her. "I'm sorry, Merry. I should have listened to you."

"Merry, I need you to stay still until we can clear you for fractures and a head injury," Dr. Katy chimed in. "Right now, we're going to get you entered into the computer system as a patient."

Merry's eyes widened. "A patient? But I have to work!"

"Not happening," Zack said, his voice harsher than he intended. He wasn't angry at Merry, but at himself. He forced himself to speak to her in a gentle tone. "You're going to do whatever the doctor tells you, okay?"

Dr. Katy nodded her approval and walked away, leaving the two of them alone.

Merry's amber gaze bored into his. "Sounds like you're not giving me much of a choice," she finally muttered.

"I know, and I'm sorry. I feel terrible about what happened, but we need to know how badly you're injured."

Zack resisted the urge to brush her reddish gold hair away from her cheek. He couldn't afford to get emotionally involved with Merry, no matter how much he liked her. Even now, well past two years after he lost his wife and daughter within six months of each other, he fought to keep his emotions in a deep freeze. Why were they thawing now, for his sister's friend, Merry Haines? It wasn't fair, since he had no intention of getting emotionally involved ever again.

"Is Leonard okay?" Merry asked.

He admired her ability to worry about the big man who'd knocked her around like a rag doll. "He'll be fine. They managed to get him medicated and back into his room."

Merry closed her eyes for a moment, and the tiny pucker between her brows made him realize she was in pain. "Poor Leonard, it's not his fault."

As a police officer, Zack interacted with many people with psychiatric issues. But he had to admit that Leonard was one of the worst he'd ever seen. That moment when Merry had stepped in front of Leonard, trying to reason with him was burned into Zach's memory. She'd reminded him of a slender David facing down Goliath, except her sling-shot was a cup of chocolate pudding. Pudding that was now splattered all over the wall.

"You should have gotten out of the way," he said in a weary tone. "The man is more than twice your size."

"Normally, Leonard likes me," Merry whispered. "I thought I could get through to him. I didn't want him to get hurt."

He wasn't sure what to say since he knew very well it was his fault that Leonard lost control.

Zack scrubbed his hands over his face. He was due to return to Madison with the evidence he'd come to collect, but he couldn't bring himself to leave Merry like this. Especially since his sister, Julie, wasn't around to help. He remembered talking to Merry at Julie and Derek's wedding and, at the time, she'd mentioned she didn't have any family in the area.

Zack pulled up a chair next to Merry's bedside and sat down. Her eyes drifted closed, deep brackets of pain pulling at the corners of her mouth. Her face was incredibly pale, each freckle standing out starkly against her skin.

As much as he didn't want to get involved, he couldn't make himself leave. At least, not until he knew she was all right. She looked far too helpless lying there on the bed.

He closed his eyes and pressed the heels of his palms into his eyes. Once he would have prayed for Merry's recovery, but not anymore.

Unfortunately, God had stopped listening to him a long time ago.

2

Merry pried open her eyelids, squinting against the pain reverberating through her skull. For a moment she had no idea where she was, though the overhead light was confusingly familiar. It took several minutes for her to realize she was on the wrong side of a hospital bed. And in the ER, the department she worked in, no less.

Very slowly, she turned her head toward the door. She was shocked to see Zack Crain sitting in a chair next to her bed, cradling his head in his hands, looking ironically vulnerable considering she was the one wearing a hospital gown.

"Zack? What's wrong?"

His head snapped up, his piercing green gaze capturing hers. A flash of relief flittered across his features. "You're awake," he said, rising to his feet.

"Barely. What happened?" she asked, putting her hand to her throbbing temple.

"You don't remember?" His eyes betrayed his concern. "Are you feeling okay?"

"Sore," she murmured, downplaying her pain as much as possible. "I remember some things, but parts of my memory is nothing more than a blur. How long have I been sleeping? Where's the doctor?"

Zach reached over to push the call light lying beside her. "You've been out for about ninety minutes or so. I'm sure Dr. Katy and Janelle will be here soon."

The image of Leonard shoving her aside flashed in her memory. "What happened to Leonard? He didn't have to go to the psych hospital in Madison did he?"

"I don't think so. He calmed down after they gave him a shot." Zack's dark green eyes reflected his guilt. "I feel awful about what happened, Merry."

She tried to smile, even though even that much movement made her head pound. "I told you it wasn't your fault."

"I should have listened to you," he persisted, his fingers tightly gripping the side rail of her bed. "I should have left the room right away."

She hated to watch him beating himself up like this. "Zack, it was probably too late. Leonard has cop radar. He can sense you guys a mile away. But it's not his fault, either. He had a bad experience several years ago and has associated police with pain ever since." She shifted in the bed, and winced. "I need to get up."

"Not a good idea," Zack said, putting a hand on her right shoulder to keep her from trying to sit up. Sharp pain stabbed the upper part of her left chest, and she vaguely remembered hitting the nursing station on that side.

"Don't move until the doctor says you can," Zack cautioned. "There was talk about a possible broken clavicle to go along with your concussion."

"Broken clavicle?" She couldn't mask her horror. A

concussion was bad enough, but a broken clavicle could keep her off work for up to eight weeks.

"They don't know for sure," Zack admitted. "They did X-rays along with the CT scan of your head."

"How's our star patient?" Dr. Katy asked cheerfully as she walked into the room.

Merry had been a patient in the hospital once before, and she didn't much care for it now. Did she sound as condescending when she talked to patients? If so, she needed to change her approach.

"Tell me about my injuries," Merry said, reminding herself that Dr. Katy was a great ER doctor, one she'd always respected. "Zack mentioned something about a broken collarbone?"

One of her colleagues, Janelle, came into the room and stood beside Dr. Katy.

"You have a cracked collarbone on your left side and a concussion," Dr. Katy informed her. "The fracture is not displaced so it should heal up fine on its own. We'll give you a sling to wear when you're up. And I'd like to keep you overnight so we can monitor your concussion."

"Overnight?" Staying here as a patient was the last thing she wanted to do. "But I'm dog-sitting Ace for Julie and Derek. He can't stay home alone."

"When did Julie and Derek get a dog?" Zack asked.

Thinking hurt, but she managed to count backwards. "About two months ago. One of their neighbors passed away so they adopted Ace rather than send him to the humane society. He's very well trained and Lexi adores him."

"Merry, being monitored here is important," Dr. Katy chimed in. "The bleeding on the back of your head has stopped and we don't think you'll need stitches. But still, you know how tricky a head injury can be." Dr. Katy raised her brow. "Are you willing? I'd like to call upstairs to reserve a bed for you."

"Stay. I'll take care of Ace," Zack promised.

Nausea rolled through her belly, a lousy side effect of her concussion. As much as she didn't want to stay, she knew that even minor head injuries could change into something worse. She needed to be smart about her health.

"All right," she agreed, swallowing hard and praying she wouldn't humiliate herself further by throwing up in front of Zack. "I'll stay."

"Great. We'll get things going on our end," Dr. Katy said in a cheerful tone that somehow managed to grate on Merry's nerves. She was really, really, going to change her bedside manner from now on. Dr. Katy left the room, presumably to get her admitted to a nursing unit. Janelle did a quick set of vitals before following Dr. Katy out of the room. Merry wasn't exactly sad to see them leave. She wanted to close her eyes and shut everyone out, but she needed to make sure Zack took care of Ace.

She glanced up at him. "I've been staying with Ace at Julie and Derek's townhouse because my apartment building doesn't allow pets. If you could stay with him there, I'd appreciate it."

"Okay. I need the key." At her blank expression, Zack grimaced. "Let me guess, the place isn't locked up."

She flashed a weary smile. "What do you think? You know there's hardly any crime in Crystal Lake."

Zack scowled but didn't argue. "Is the other side of the townhouse still vacant?"

"Yes." Merry didn't mention that she'd planned to ask if she could rent the place from Julie until her friend explained how she and Derek were putting the entire building up for sale next year. They wanted to build their own home on the lake. Not that she blamed them, but there was no way she could afford to buy the entire townhouse even if she could manage to rent out the other half, which of course was no guarantee.

"Okay, I'll check on Ace," Zack said, looking down at his watch. "I have to run the evidence back to Madison first and finish my shift, but I'll head over as soon as I'm finished."

"Thanks," she whispered. She wasn't sure she could maintain her composure for much longer. She silently prayed for strength.

"Take care, Merry," Zack said, his tone surprisingly gentle. "I'll be back later to check on you."

She wanted to tell him he didn't need to come back, but she closed her eyes, still fighting against the swirling nausea. By the time she opened her eyes again, Zack was gone.

And despite how terrible she felt, she found herself looking forward to seeing him again.

ZACK MADE the trip back to Madison in record time, without speeding. He reported in with the evidence he'd collected, and then went out to finish up his shift, pulling over several speeders and one OWI before heading home. It was Thursday and he was off the weekend, but he was scheduled to work tomorrow morning, unless he could find someone else to pick up his shift.

He didn't have to make too many phone calls to get someone to pick up his Friday hours. Over the past few years he'd buried himself in work, taking any and all shifts offered up so he didn't have to think about everything he'd lost. One of the guys he routinely covered for was happy to return the favor.

Swallowing hard, he steeled himself against the usual wave of anger, but surprisingly, the emotion didn't hit him with the same force it had in the past. It was a little over two years ago since he'd lost his wife and his daughter to cancer within six months of each other, and he'd hovered on the brink of despair for a long time.

It didn't seem right that he was slowly getting over the loss. Suzanne and Amelia had once been the center of his world. He had no intention of ever replacing them in his heart.

But life trudged on, and inexplicably the pain eased from sharp and breathtaking to a low constant ache. He stood in the tiny kitchen of his apartment, forcing himself to remember Suzanne's face as she held their dying daughter. The image was fuzzy, and he was irritated to realize that Merry's pale face flashed in his mind with far more clarity.

No. He wasn't going there. Merry was his sister's friend, nothing more. He'd enjoyed talking to her at Julie and Derek's wedding but was determined to keep his distance from anything remotely romantic. She was a friend, and that was the only reason he was pitching in to help out. Especially since her injury was mostly his fault.

He changed out of his uniform and pulled on comfortable clothes—well-worn jeans and a T-shirt, both hanging loosely on his lanky frame. He'd returned to the gym, trying to gain back some of the weight he'd lost after burying his family but, so far, he was still a good thirty pounds under his normal weight.

Zack packed spare clothes in a small duffel bag, tossed in his tablet which contained the latest legal thriller, and then tucked his badge and his gun inside. He hooked the duffel over his shoulder, grabbed his keys off the table and headed back outside to his black pick-up truck. Since he was officially off the next three days, he didn't want to drive the squad car. He realized it had been too long, since Derek and Julie's wedding, that he'd had some downtime. As he headed out of town, he filled up his gas tank, wincing at the ridiculously high prices, before heading out to the interstate.

The summer sun was high in the sky and a cool breeze filtered in through his open driver's side window. For a moment he felt almost happy, or at least not sad. He told himself that his lighthearted mood was probably because he didn't have to work for the next few days. He was clearly overdue for some rest and relaxation.

He tuned in the radio to his favorite country station and let the twang of music wash over him as he headed out to Crystal Lake. He and Julie had grown up there, and the small town was chock full of memories, both good and bad. Growing up they'd had a great time, waterskiing and tubing on the lake. He'd met Suzanne in college, and they'd gotten married as soon as he'd graduated. They'd made their home in Crystal Lake until cancer struck, not just once but twice, stealing the two people he'd loved the most.

He'd moved away after losing Suzanne and Amelia, but if he were honest with himself, he'd admit that Madison just wasn't home.

Of course, he'd never have a home again, so it didn't matter much that the city housing the state capitol was still as foreign to him now as it had been two years ago when he first moved. Some of the guys he worked with still razzed him when he managed to get lost.

His truck quickly ate up the miles, and he made it to Crystal Lake near dinnertime. He drove down Main Street, smiling a little when he saw Rose's Café. Josie ran the place now, and he wouldn't mind stopping there to get something to eat. But first he had to head over to Derek and Julie's townhouse to take care of Ace.

His sister's home was located a few minutes outside of town, one of the few rental properties with lakefront access. He pulled into the driveway and climbed from the truck, gratefully stretching out his legs.

He headed up to the front door, hoping that Ace would somehow recognize him as a friend rather than a foe. He could hear the dog start barking the minute he climbed up onto the front porch, and he wished he'd kept his uniform on since it was entirely possible that Merry's scent would calm the animal down.

"Easy, Ace, good dog," he called. He opened the front door, and the black lab stood his ground, barking furiously as if protecting the home from an invader.

Zack tensed, hoping the animal wouldn't leap up and sink his teeth in. He considered lowering himself to the stoop, so that his body was less threatening, but wasn't sure if that would be a good idea if he had to run.

"Easy, Ace. I'm Julie's brother, and I'm not going to hurt you." He felt a bit ridiculous talking to the animal, but he wasn't sure what else to do. He didn't dare take his eyes off the lab, and slowly lowered himself into a crouch. "I'm a friend, Ace. I'm a friend."

The dog stopped barking, and Zack let out a tiny sigh of relief. Ace came outside, sniffing the air as if trying to determine if he approved of Zack's scent. Zack wished he'd spent more time at his sister's house so the dog would recognize him. Was four months too long for his scent to linger?

"Easy boy," he said again, holding out his hand palm up. "Do you want to smell me some more?"

Ace stretched his neck out, his nose still sniffing the air. After what seemed like forever, the dog crept closer and sniffed his hand. Zack stayed still, unwilling to make any sudden moves. Maybe there was some of Merry's scent still clinging to his skin, because Ace began to wag his tail in a sign of welcome.

"That's it, boy, we're good." Zack stroked the dog lightly, and then stood up as the lab bounded out to do his business.

"Okay, I think we've made it past the first hurdle, boy," he said, still talking to the dog since there wasn't anyone else around. For the first time he thought that having a pet to come home to might not be a bad idea. He'd chosen to live a lonely life, a decision he didn't regret. But a dog would make his self-imposed isolation more bearable.

"Come on, Ace, let's go inside," he called. He stepped back up on the porch and opened the front door, hoping the dog would get the message.

But Ace ran over to the bushes around the corner of the townhouse, sniffing furiously along the ground, growling low in his throat.

"What's wrong, boy?" Had the dog found some sort of animal hiding under there? If so, he hoped it wasn't a skunk. That was a nightmare he did not need. Zack crossed over to the dog. "What's wrong, Ace? What did you find?"

No signs of an animal that he could see, but then he caught a glimpse of a footprint in the mud, almost directly beneath the bedroom window.

He narrowed his gaze, kneeling beside the footprint that looked to be relatively fresh, considering a band of severe thunderstorms had moved through just two days ago. He couldn't see the imprint of a tread, and from the shape of the print he thought it was likely a boot had made the impression rather than an athletic shoe, a size eleven or twelve at best guess. He wanted to get a ruler to use as a reference point for the footprint.

He rocked back on his heels, glancing around the area, searching for anything that seemed out of place. He didn't know for sure how long Derek and Julie had been gone, but it seemed odd that the boot print would belong to Derek anyway. The window looked to be in perfectly good shape, with no evidence of recent repairs.

"Good job," he murmured to Ace, who came up beside him. He leaned down and gave the dog a thorough rub. "Good boy."

He went into the house and searched for a ruler. Then he returned to the site, setting the twelve inch ruler against the boot print, first lengthwise, and then measuring the width, taking several photos with his phone.

While he was glad that Merry had Ace here to keep an eye on her, he didn't like the thought of someone creeping up to the bedroom window, trying to look inside.

If the mystery Peeping Tom planned to return while Zack was here, he'd be in for a big surprise. Because Zack wasn't going to take a crime like this lightly, especially if Merry or his sister, Julie, were the intended victims.

MERRY COULDN'T BELIEVE how uncomfortable hospital beds were. How in the world did they expect patients to get better when they were resting on a bag of rocks that masqueraded as a mattress?

She never should have agreed to stay. If she were back at

the townhouse she'd be resting in a softer bed and would have Ace for company.

"Time for your neuro check," Gail the floor nurse said as she entered the room.

Merry tried to smile, knowing her bad temper wasn't the staff's fault. All this time she thought doctors always made the worst patients, but maybe nurses ran a close second. "Okay."

Gail ran through the routine, one that had been repeated every two hours since she'd regained consciousness.

"How are my pupils?" she asked, when Gail finished peering into her eyes with a penlight.

"Equal and reactive," Gail responded. "Do you know where you are?"

"Hope County Hospital," Merry responded. "My name is Merry Haines and today is August eighth, twenty-thirteen."

"I'm sure this is getting annoying by now," Gail said sympathetically.

"Oh yeah." She preferred Gail's honesty over the false cheerfulness. Or maybe it wasn't false, but dealing with perky cheerfulness when your head felt like it was going to explode wasn't easy.

"You get to advance to full liquids for dinner," Gail said. "Let me know when you want me to call for a tray."

Her earlier nausea had faded after drinking broth and eating Jell-O, a good sign that she was getting better, not worse. "Now is good. It's already after six." And visiting hours were over at eight o'clock, not that she'd been watching the clock for Zack to show up or anything. She was grateful enough that he was taking care of Ace.

"All right. Is there anything else I can get you?" Gail asked.

"A softer mattress?" Merry forced a smile. "No, thanks. I'm fine."

"I'm sure it's not easy for you being a patient here," Gail said. "I don't think I'd like it much either."

So her bad temper was noticeable. What was wrong with her? Usually she was always the one with the positive glass-half-full outlook on life. She needed to get over herself already.

"Yeah, I wouldn't recommend it," she said to Gail. "But seriously, thanks for everything."

"You're welcome. Expect your tray in about an hour, okay?"

"Sounds good." Merry shifted in the bed, trying to find a more comfortable position. Maybe it was a good thing that Zack hadn't returned. With any luck she'd feel more human by morning and be well enough for discharge. Although what she'd do with herself for eight weeks, was something else entirely. The thought of sitting idle in her apartment was far too depressing.

There was a knock at her door. "Come in," she called, expecting her dinner tray.

Zack poked his head in. "Are you up for a wheelchair ride?" he asked.

She shouldn't be so happy to see him, but she was. She wondered if he knew she was on bed rest or maybe he just assumed she needed a wheelchair. "I guess, why?"

"It's a surprise." Zack thrust the door open and pushed a wheelchair through. "Do you need help?"

She hoped he didn't notice her blush. "I can get up on my own," she muttered.

He stood holding the wheelchair steady as she stood at the side of the bed, grateful that she was wearing a robe so that her backside wouldn't be flapping in the breeze, and then turned to sit back down. She tugged at her shoulder sling, trying to make her arm more comfortable.

"Ready?" Zack asked, grinning like a fool.

His smile was contagious. "Absolutely."

He wheeled her down the hall and into the elevator. When they reached the lobby level, he pushed her straight through the revolving doors and into the fresh air.

"This is wonderful," she said, lifting her face to the warm summer breeze and taking a deep breath, enjoying the strong scent of lilacs. "Thanks so much for bringing me out here."

He pushed her down the sidewalk until he found a shady spot beneath a tree. He set the brakes on her wheelchair. "Wait here, okay?"

"Sure." She frowned when he hurried away to the large surface parking lot. What was he doing?

A few minutes later, he returned with Ace trotting at his side, looking downright docile on his leash. She couldn't prevent the huge smile that bloomed as they approached.

"I figured you needed a friend," he said. "And I didn't want to leave him home alone, again."

Zack let go of the leash and Ace ran over to her, wagging his entire body as well as his tail in welcome before he tried to crawl into her lap.

It had been so long since anyone had done something this nice for her. And the fact that Zack had gone out of his way to cheer her up meant far more than it should have.

She knew Zack was still mourning his deceased wife and daughter, so getting emotionally involved with him was not an option.

No matter how much she wanted to.

3

Merry grimaced as the dog licked her face. "No, Ace, knock it off," she said, trying to avoid another doggie kiss.

"Down, Ace," Zack said firmly and, amazingly, the dog sat back on his haunches, his tongue lolling out of his mouth as he looked at them.

"Wow, he must think you sound like Derek. He doesn't behave like that for me." Merry reached out to scratch Ace behind the ears. "Thanks so much for bringing him. Ace is just what I needed to cheer me up."

"Pets are good at that, aren't they?" Zack bent over to pick up Ace's leash, and then looped it over the arm of her wheelchair.

"Yes, they are. I appreciate the last minute dog-sitting duty, too."

"It's no problem," Zack said. "Although I have to admit, it was touch and go when I first got to the house, while he decided whether or not I was one of the good guys."

"Oh no, I never thought of that," Merry said, battling a wave of regret. Why hadn't she considered that possibility?

Especially since she knew Ace was a good guard dog. "See? I knew I should have insisted on going home. At least then I could have made the transition easier for you."

"I'm glad you're staying," he said. "Otherwise I'd have to worry about you."

The thought of Zack worrying made her heart flip, and she took a deep breath in an attempt to hide her reaction. "I'm fine. Dr. Katy was being overly cautious."

"Smart doctor. So what time do you think they'll let you go tomorrow?" Zack asked, changing the subject.

She shook her head. "I'm not sure, but the sooner the better as far as I'm concerned. I have my car here, so I'll be able to drive myself home. Thankfully, I don't have a stick shift and I'm right handed, so driving shouldn't be a problem. What about you? Do you work tomorrow?"

"Nope, I have the next three days off." Zack looked so relaxed and content that she could barely reconcile the man sitting on the bench beside her with the man she'd chatted with at Julie's wedding. Of course, it could be that watching his sister get married, while knowing he'd already lost his wife and daughter, had been extraordinarily difficult.

"I'm glad to hear you have some time off," she said, petting Ace, who'd flopped down at her feet. "I imagine your job is stressful."

"So is yours," he pointed out. "I think you should have a cop stationed in your ER all the time, considering some of the stuff that's happened there."

She couldn't argue his logic. They had a shoot-out in the trauma room of the ER over a year ago, and now this latest issue with Leonard. Both incidents were very much out of the ordinary for Hope County Hospital.

Her stomach rumbled and she thought about her dinner

tray waiting for her. "I should probably head back inside," she murmured. "I'm so lucky, I get to eat soup for dinner."

"Just soup?" Zack echoed with a wry grimace. "Do you want me to sneak you in a burger from Rose's Café?"

She laughed and shook her head. "That's a nice offer, but no thanks. I've been feeling sick to my stomach since this morning, so going slow is probably a better option right now. By tomorrow I should be able to have normal food."

His smile faded, and she regretted reminding him about her accident. "I understand," he said. "Give me a minute to put Ace back in my truck, and then I'll wheel you back upstairs."

It was on the tip of her tongue to tell him not to bother, until she realized she couldn't propel herself with one arm. She waited for Zack, thinking there nothing worse than feeling helpless.

A glimpse of a red-haired man flashed along the edge of her vision. She instinctively froze, her heart pounding in her chest. She forced herself to swivel around in her seat to sweep her gaze over the area. Her entire body was tense, until she saw the redhead amongst a group of staff members, all wearing scrubs, walking out toward their cars. She let out a heavy sigh. It was seven-thirty, the end of shift for some of the staff who worked twelve hours at a time.

Idiot, she scolded herself. The redhead she'd glimpsed was not Blake. She'd stopped looking over her shoulder, searching for her ex-boyfriend a year ago, so why was she suddenly doing that again now? Because she'd been injured and was feeling vulnerable? Maybe. The last time she'd been in the hospital as a patient had been after Blake attacked her.

Regardless, she had to stop this nonsense and move forward with her life. She hadn't been out on a date in forever, although, between her job and volunteering in the church choir, she managed to keep busy. Truthfully, she didn't have any desire to get back out in the dating scene.

Blake had seemed so nice and normal at first. To discover his true nature had been a horrifying shock.

She didn't want to think about Blake any more. No doubt, feeling helpless had brought her old fears back to the surface. She pushed the old memories away with an effort, catching sight of Zack jogging back over, secretly relieved and grateful that he hadn't been there to witness her moment of panic.

She already felt pathetic enough, being injured and sitting in a wheelchair. The sooner she got out of the hospital, the better.

"All set?" he asked as he bent down to release the brakes of the wheelchair.

"Sure thing."

He pushed her back inside, neither one of them saying much on the trip up to her room.

"Thanks again," she said, breaking the moment of awkwardness. "Both for bringing Ace to visit me and for keeping an eye on him tonight."

"I don't mind," Zack said. "I'll see you tomorrow."

She lifted her eyebrows in surprise. "Tomorrow?"

He nodded. "I've decided to spend the weekend in Crystal Lake. I haven't been out on my boat in ages."

Merry stared at him in shock, never expecting that he'd be staying at the townhouse, too. But really, what could she say? Zack was Julie's brother, and the speedboat moored up in the boat lift was his. He had every right to stay at his sister's townhouse.

Unless he was doing this out of a misplaced sense of guilt?

"Zack, I hope you're not hanging around just because of what happened with Leonard. I've told you several times it wasn't your fault."

He shrugged in a way that made her think he was still wrestling with guilt. "To be honest, I haven't had time off in months, and I'm looking forward to spending the weekend on the lake."

Merry knew that Julie would be ecstatic to know that her brother was planning to spend the weekend relaxing on his boat. Julie's concern over her brother's emotional state was no secret. His taking time off work to play on the water seemed like a huge step in the right direction.

Who was she to argue?

"I'm glad," she murmured. "You deserve a little fun."

His gaze darkened for a moment, before his expression cleared. "Goodnight, Merry." Zack flashed a crooked smile before leaving.

She ate her cream soup, Jell-O and pudding, trying not to get too excited about spending the weekend with Zack. Not that he'd indicated they'd actually spend any time together. With her lingering headache and her left arm in a sling, she wasn't going to be up for doing much, anyway.

She had to remember that Zack needed a friend, nothing more. But to be honest, she wouldn't mind having him as a friend, too.

ZACK WOKE up the next morning with Ace nudging him, feeling oddly refreshed despite spending the night in one of the twin beds that were *not* designed for a man of his size.

He blinked and stared at the ceiling for a moment, realizing he hadn't dreamed about Suzanne and Amelia in several months. Relief warred with guilt. He didn't want to forget them.

Ace whined and yelped to get his attention.

"Okay, okay, I coming." Zack swung out of the small bed and staggered through the townhouse toward the patio door in the open-concept kitchen and living area. The moment he slid the door open, Ace leaped outside.

"Ace!" he called, hoping the dog wouldn't decide to run off. Since he was dressed in a pair of running shorts and a T-shirt, he headed outside to keep an eye on the lab.

He needn't have worried. The dog did his business, and then loped back up to where Zack stood near the front of the house. Ace dropped a tennis ball on the ground and glanced up at him with a hopeful expression in his doggy eyes.

"Why do I feel like I'm going to regret this?" he asked as he bent over to pick up the ball. He tossed it high in the air, using his former high school baseball skills to make sure it didn't drop into the water.

Ace ran, leaped up and grabbed the ball in his jaw as he landed. The dog ran around in a tight circle for a minute before dashing back over to Zack, dropping down on his haunches and keeping the ball locked in his mouth.

"Neat trick," he said, smiling down at Ace. "Obviously you're in the mood to play, but I need to shower, shave and get dressed first." The last thing he needed was for Merry to come home while he still had a bed-head.

The thought pulled him up short. Since when did he care what Merry thought of him? He shouldn't care what anyone thought of the way he looked. He wasn't here to impress anyone. Least of all a woman.

Determined to prove to himself that he wasn't vain, Zack bent down and gently tugged the ball from the dog's mouth before sending it flying up in the air again and again. On the fourth time, when he put too much muscle behind the throw, sending it out over the lake, Ace didn't hesitate to jump into the water to swim out for the ball that bobbed up and down in the lake.

The water looked cool and inviting. Zack stared at the lake for a moment. Why not? He ran down the grassy embankment and jumped off the end of the pier, grabbing onto his knees so that his bottom hit the water, making a huge cannonball splash.

The cold water stole his breath, but when he shot back up to the surface, he couldn't help letting out a whoop. "Doesn't that feel great, boy?"

Ace swam over to him, the ball clenched between his teeth. Zack propelled himself toward the pier and climbed up the short ladder. Since Ace couldn't climb the ladder, the dog headed toward the shoreline to get out of the lake. Ace stood and shook his entire body, sending droplets of water in all directions.

Zack ducked his head to avoid the worst of Ace's shower. When he turned back, he saw Merry standing on the back patio, wearing her work scrubs and the arm sling. Her wide smile spiked his pulse.

"Looks like fun," she called.

It took several minutes to find his voice. "How did you manage to get discharged so early?" he asked, striving to sound casual as he walked up the lawn, water running off his clothes, to meet her.

Her grin widened. "Special treatment and a threat to leave against medical advice if they didn't let me go."

He searched her gaze, noticing the remnants of pain hidden in her eyes. "How's your head?"

"Still attached to my body as far as I can tell." She bent down to pet a very wet Ace, grimacing when he brushed up against her scrubs.

"Have you eaten breakfast?" Zack asked, tugging Ace away from her. "I was about to make some bacon and eggs, and I have more than enough to share."

He knew he was sunk when her eyes lit up with gratitude. "That would be awesome. The hospital food wasn't exactly inspiring."

"All right, give me some time to shower and change. Ace, stay," he commanded in a stern tone.

The dog flopped down on the grass, rolling around on his back as if the ground could help dry him off. Zack shook his head with amusement and went back inside the townhouse.

He found himself hurrying through his shower, and then nicked himself shaving. He dabbed at the small cut, telling himself he was an idiot.

Merry had been home for only five minutes and already he'd offered to cook her breakfast. This was supposed to be a nice relaxing weekend, not a potential date with his sister's friend and colleague. He needed to stay focused.

Because if he wasn't careful, he was going to find himself in over his head in no time.

Merry headed back inside her side of the townhouse to make a pot of coffee. She'd been up since six o'clock in the morning, having showered at the hospital. Thankfully, Carrie, her day shift nurse, had brought her a clean pair of scrubs and had helped her comb and dry her hair after her shower. Merry had been forced to ask Carrie to pull her hair back in a simple ponytail since she couldn't manage to do even that much one-handed. Luckily, her reddish gold hair had a bit of a natural curl.

The next six to eight weeks weren't going to be easy, she admitted grimly as she filled the glass carafe with water and carried it over to the coffee maker. Even the simplest tasks took twice as long as normal.

At least she had Ace to keep her company for the weekend. And Zack.

When the coffee finished brewing, she balanced her cup in her injured hand, making her way outside so she could sit on the patio overlooking the lake. Ace padded over to greet her, giving her a lick before dropping at her feet.

As she stared out over the water, she sighed, thinking that being off work for eight weeks wasn't going to help her save any money for a place of her own. She wondered if maybe she should ask Julie to rent out the vacant townhouse. A year of being on the lake was better than nothing, and maybe by then she'd have enough money saved to buy the place.

If she could work enough extra shifts. And if she could manage to save her money. Once she was cleared to return to full duty.

When she heard Zack moving around in the kitchen making breakfast, she got up and crossed over to head inside. "What do you need help with?" she asked.

"Nothing at all, just sit down and relax." He barely looked at her as he spoke, as if making bacon and eggs took all his attention.

No sense in staying where she wasn't wanted. "Do you drink coffee?" she asked.

That caught his attention. "Of course. Who doesn't?" he asked perplexed.

He made her laugh, without even trying. "I'm sure there's someone in the world who doesn't," she teased. "But I made a fresh pot next door. I'll bring a cup over for you."

Fifteen minutes later, Zack poked his head out the screen door. "Breakfast is ready."

It didn't take long to bring the plates filled with bacon, eggs and toast outside. She topped off their coffee, and then sat down and bowed her head.

"Dear Lord, thank You for providing this food to eat and guide us on Your chosen path as we enjoy this beautiful day. Amen."

She lifted her head shocked, to see Zack's expressionless face as he stared out over the lake. Her heart sank with the knowledge that he hadn't bothered to bow his head or attempt to pray.

It made her sad to realize he'd turned his back on God.

Her appetite faded, but she forced herself to eat, taking a bite of the crispy bacon. "This is delicious, thanks."

He sighed and reached for his fork. "I forgot what it was like to share a meal with a Christian."

She felt worse, knowing that Zack didn't consider himself a Christian any more. Julie mentioned that Zack hadn't been to church since his wife and daughter died. She wished there was a way to convince him that God could help support him through this difficult time in his life.

"You're still a Christian, Zack," she said. "God hasn't given up on you, even if you've given up on Him."

Zack didn't respond, eating his food as they were in a race and he wanted to finish first. The easy camaraderie they'd shared evaporated and she had no idea how to get it back.

Did she even want to get it back?

Yes. Yes, she did.

She stared out at the lake, watching the water-skiers and tubers having fun as they flew behind their respective speed boats. Zack would likely head out onto the water as soon as they finished eating, no doubt anxious to get away from her.

She told herself it didn't matter, that Zack was here to relax and have fun. If he didn't want to talk about his faith or church, she wouldn't push.

"When did Julie and Derek leave?" Zack asked.

She was startled by the change in subject. "Tuesday morning, why?"

"You've been here since Tuesday?" he persisted.

She shrugged, using her fork to toy with her eggs. "Yes, I stayed over on Monday night because they were hitting the road early. They dropped Lexi off at her grandparents' house in St. Louis before they headed for a cabin they rented in the Smokey Mountains."

"And Tuesday night the thunderstorms came through, right?" he asked.

"Yes. Why? What is this about?"

Zack was silent for a minute. "Do you see that fishing boat out there on the water?"

Fishing boat? She looked over in the direction he indicated and froze when she saw a man with a baseball cap on his head, fishing not far from the end of their pier.

Her fork clattered to her plate as her fingers went numb. Beneath the blue baseball cap, she could see the thick, bright red hair.

Blake!

4

"No!" Merry stumbled to her feet, nearly falling over in her haste to get away from the table. This couldn't be happening. How had Blake found her?

Zack jumped up to catch her, his strong arms holding her steady. "Merry, what's wrong?"

She shook her head, unable to answer. Trembling with fear, she peered over his shoulder and stared out at the lake, trying to make sure that the guy was actually Blake. But the man in the fishing boat had turned around and was moving steadily away so she could only see his back.

And another glimpse of his red hair.

"Merry, who was that guy?" Zack persisted.

"I—I don't know," she whispered. Was it Blake? Or was she imagining things again? Every guy with red hair wasn't Blake. Hadn't she made the same mistake last evening outside the hospital? Yet, despite the summer heat she was chilled to the bone.

Zack must have known she was cold because he pulled her into his arms and hugged her. For a moment she rested her head on his shoulder, grateful for his strength and his warmth. Just inhaling his musky, male scent brought her a sense of calmness.

Please, Lord, keep me safe from Blake. Please!

"Let's sit down and finish our breakfast, okay?" Zack murmured.

She forced herself to pull away from his embrace. One last glance at the lake confirmed the fishing boat was long gone. Merry sank into her seat and picked up her fork, although her appetite had completely vanished.

"Merry, you need to tell me what happened," Zack pressed as he sat down beside her. "Has someone been bothering you? Maybe an old boyfriend?"

Ace came over and stuck his head into her lap, as if he sensed she was upset. She stroked the dog's black, silky fur, trying to bolster her flagging courage. As much as she didn't like to talk about her past, she knew Zack deserved some sort of answer.

"I haven't dated anyone in over two years," she said finally. "Since I lived in Minneapolis."

If he was shocked by her lack of social life, he didn't let on. "So you haven't noticed anyone following you lately?" Zack asked.

"No, I haven't." Suddenly she was angry with him. "Why don't you just get to the point, Zack? You're the one who noticed the guy in the fishing boat. Do you think he's following me? Why do I get the feeling there's something you're not telling me?"

Zack grimaced. "You're right. I did notice that guy in the boat. I thought it was a little odd he chose to fish right here amidst the boaters, tubers and skiers churning up the water. Early morning hours are best, and any serious fisherman would know that. I thought he seemed suspicious."

She didn't understand what he was trying to say, especially since Zack couldn't possibly know about Blake. "But why in the world would you think some guy in a fishing boat is watching me?"

"Yesterday afternoon, when I came here to let Ace out, he went sniffing and growling by the side of the house. I thought he found an animal or something, but when I went over there, I saw a footprint in the soft soil beneath the bedroom window."

Merry felt the blood drain from her face. "A footprint?" she repeated hoarsely.

"Yeah. So when I saw that guy in the fishing boat right next to our pier, I became suspicious. Especially when you seemed to recognize him. So now it's your turn, Merry. Tell me who he is."

She shivered, and couldn't help wondering if the man in the boat really was Blake after all? Would he really have come to find her after two long years? And if so, why? Surely, he couldn't still be obsessed with her?

She didn't want to believe the man was Blake, but she was equally afraid to ignore the potential threat. She pushed her plate away and struggled to her feet. "Show me the footprint."

Zack stood and walked across the patio, around Julie's small vegetable garden, to the south side of the house. She followed with Ace trotting along beside her.

"Right there," Zack said, as he indicated the area beneath the bedroom window where she'd been sleeping the past few nights.

She crept closer until she could see the distinct footprint in the soil. Seeing the evidence for herself only made her feel sick to her stomach.

"I've taken pictures of the print, and I'd be happy to help you file a police report if necessary," Zack was saying.

She swung around to face him. "How can I file a police report? I didn't get a good look at the guy in the boat, so I can't describe his face."

"But you know who he is, right?" Zack said gently.

She let out her breath in a loud sigh, knowing that Zack's cop instincts were not going to let this go. "It could be a guy I once dated, Blake Caruthers. He has bright red hair, just like the guy in the boat. But he lives in Minneapolis, or he did the last time I saw him. Don't we need proof that he's really here, following me, before we go to the police?"

"It wouldn't hurt to file a restraining order against him," Zack said.

She shook her head, a sense of helplessness washing over her. "There's no point. I already have a restraining order against him and it's active for another two years. Besides, in my experience, a restraining order isn't worth the paper it's printed on."

Merry turned and walked away, unable to bear talking about Blake any more. If he was really here in Crystal Lake, then she'd have no choice but to pick up and move again.

Although that wouldn't be easy, since she wasn't able to work for the next six to eight weeks. Not to mention packing or lifting boxes. She'd have to wait for her collarbone to heal.

And by then she could easily be dead. Because if Blake was really after her all this time, she knew he wouldn't stop until he satisfied his need for revenge.

Zack followed Merry to the patio, his thoughts whirling. Granted, he was the one who'd found the footprint and noticed the guy in the fishing boat, but he was still shocked to know Merry was really being stalked.

"I need you to tell me everything you know about this guy, Blake Caruthers," he commanded when she sat back down at the table. "I'll start investigating him, immediately."

Merry grimaced and shook her head. "I don't want to go into all this now."

Zack battled a flash of temper. "Merry, we can't just sit here and pretend this isn't happening. This guy, Blake, could be dangerous. I'll start investigating him, and once we prove he's not in Minneapolis any more, we can go to the sheriff's department here. Trust me, being in a small town will be an advantage. The Crystal Lake deputies will be far more concerned about protecting one of their citizens, especially a young woman like you, than any big city cop."

She lifted her brow. "Aren't you a big city cop now?"

"Don't try to change the subject," he warned, ignoring the light jab. "Because I can tell you right now, I'm not going to let this go."

"It's a long story and one that can certainly wait until later." She stood and picked up her plate, but when she turned to the sliding glass doors leading into the house, she stopped and let out a frustrated sound. "Will you open the door for me, please?"

"Sit down. I'll take care of the dishes. It's not like you can do much with one hand."

"Fine." She thrust the plate at him, and then went around to the other set of patio doors. "I'm going to rest for a while. My head is pounding." Merry didn't so much as glance at him as she went into Julie and Derek's side of the townhouse, the screen door snapping shut behind her.

Zack rubbed the back of his neck, knowing she was upset with him, but uncertain as to why. It wasn't his fault that Blake was here, following her. All he wanted to do was to help protect her.

He stacked their dirty dishes and carried them inside. He quickly washed and dried them before grabbing his tablet out of his room.

The glare of the sun made it difficult to read the tablet outside, so he stayed inside to begin a cursory search for Blake Caruthers. When Ace whined at the door, he stood up and let the dog inside.

"Good boy," he murmured, giving Ace a pat on the head. After seeing the guy in the fishing boat, he was even more grateful to have Ace around as a watch dog. He was tempted to put Ace in Merry's side of the townhouse, but didn't want to interrupt if she really was trying to get some sleep.

He surfed the internet for the next hour, trying to find anything he could about Blake Caruthers out of Minneapolis. He found a social media account for the name, but there was no photo attached to the page. According to the information on the social media account, he could see that Blake attended the University of Minnesota. He sat back in his seat, wondering if Merry had received her nursing degree at the same college. It would make sense that they'd met there.

It bothered him to think about how Merry had dated the guy. A man who'd betrayed her trust, doing something terrible enough that she was able to take out a restraining order against him. He knew for sure Blake had hurt her emotionally, but had he also hurt her physically? Sexually?

He felt sick at the thought.

Zack found a Caroline Caruthers linked to Blake's social media page. When he clicked on the picture he saw a pretty woman with bright red hair. Very different from Merry's reddish blonde but they shared similar freckles. Was Caroline Caruthers, Blake's sister? Did Merry know Caroline, too? Was it possible they were all at the University at the same time?

He scrounged around the townhouse to find paper and pencil. He caught a glimpse of Lexi's many sketchbooks and decided his niece wouldn't mind if he borrowed a few pages.

Taking notes helped keep his simmering anger at bay. If this Blake guy thought he was going to hurt Merry again, he was sorely mistaken. After Zack took notes on the scant information he'd been able to find, he searched on the public access simple case search function to find the restraining order. The information was there, but there wasn't much detail. Just that Blake Caruthers was supposed to stay at least twenty feet away from Merry Haines.

He stared at the computer, wishing he could find a way to prove Caruthers had already violated the court order. There were other violations in the system for Blake, too. Zack read each one, noting that Caruthers spent time in jail for possession of illegal drugs, theft, disorderly conduct, and breaking and entering. Obviously the guy didn't seem to learn from his mistakes.

Zack scowled and reached for his phone. He called his buddy, Colton Wallace, the guy who'd covered his shift for him.

"Cole? It's Zack."

"What's up? Are you enjoying the lake?"

"Sure am," Zack replied. It wasn't a lie, he had enjoyed his brief swim. "But I need a favor. There's a young woman in town being harassed by some guy, and she already has a restraining order against him. I found a copy on-line, but I need to know what kind of vehicle this guy is driving. Can you look up his driver's registration for me? His name is Blake Caruthers and he lives in Minneapolis, Minnesota."

"Sure." He could hear Cole typing on a keyboard in the background, each squad was equipped with a computer. "What's his date of birth?"

Zack gave the information he'd found on-line, making a mental note that Caruthers was two years older than Merry.

"Got it," Cole said.

"Give me the tag number of his vehicle."

Colton rattled off the information and Zack wrote everything down.

"He actually drives a minivan?" Zack asked incredulously.

"That's what's registered to his name, although I suppose he could have purchased a different vehicle without bothering to notify the state." There was more tapping of the computer, and then Cole let out a low whistle. "Wow, this guy has quite the rap sheet."

"I know," Zack muttered.

"You better watch your back," Cole warned. "This guy is no stranger to crime."

No kidding. And it really made him mad that Caruthers was likely out here, stalking Merry. "Thanks for the help, Cole. I really appreciate it."

"No problem. Let me know if you need anything else."

"I will." Zack disconnected the call, grimly realizing he might need Cole's help again.

He wasn't going to rest until he found Blake Caruthers, proved he violated his restraining order and sent him back to jail, locking him up where he belonged.

MERRY TOOK some ibuprofen and tried to rest, but she couldn't seem to get past the brief image of the red-haired man on the boat. She told herself that if that guy really was Blake, at least he knew she wasn't here alone. He would have seen Zack and Ace both sitting beside her on the patio.

But the knowledge wasn't exactly reassuring, since she knew all too well what Blake was capable of.

She squeezed her eyes shut, not wanting to relive the past. It was over and done. Zack was right about one thing—Blake wouldn't find it so easy to get to her here in Crystal Lake. She knew many of the deputies by name, since they often accompanied car crash victims or DUI violators to the emergency department. Plus, Julie and Derek were her friends, and Derek was one of the sheriff's deputies, too. Being on a first name basis with the police would certainly help.

With a rush she sat up in bed, making her head pound with the sudden movement. Wait a minute, she didn't have to pick up and move. She could ask Julie and Derek to allow her to rent the other half of the townhouse. Then for sure, Blake wouldn't be so brazen as to violate the restraining order. Not when Derek, another sheriff's deputy was living right next door.

Feeling calmer at having a rational and workable plan, she settled back down. She must have dozed a bit because when she opened her eyes, she realized well over an hour had passed.

The nagging headache lingering behind her eyes had faded, so she swung out of bed and made her way back into the kitchen. She poured a tall glass of sun tea, one of her favorite beverages, and looked longingly outside. Realizing that attempting to hide from Zack was just plain stupid, she forced herself to go outside to sit on the patio.

"Merry? How are you feeling?" Zack asked, as he came outside to meet her. Ace acted as if she'd been gone for days instead of hours, greeting her with a wagging tail and happy doggy kisses.

"Better," she admitted, giving Ace the attention he craved. "My headache is mostly gone."

"I'd offer to take you out on the boat, but I'm afraid that hitting the waves would make your headache come back," Zack said with regret. "But maybe we can go tomorrow, if it stays nice and doesn't rain."

She shouldn't have been so thrilled with his offhand invitation, but she was. "I'd like to go out on the boat. Couldn't we try this afternoon?"

"Tomorrow is soon enough," Zack said firmly. "You just got out of the hospital, remember?"

"I suppose you're right," she said with a sigh. She glanced out at the water, instinctively looking for the fishing boat. "Any sign of him?"

"No, but I've done a little research while you were resting," Zack admitted. "Do you know Caroline? Is she Blake's sister?"

Her mouth fell open in surprise. "How did you know?"

"I went through social media websites to find him and found her, too. I noticed you all went to college together."

She was amazed he'd found out so much information in such a short period of time. "Yes, we did."

Zack leaned forward, his gaze earnest. "Look, I don't want to upset you, but the only way I can keep you safe is if you tell me what happened."

Zack compassion was nearly palpable, and she knew

feeling embarrassed was ridiculous. It wasn't as if she'd asked for Blake to become obsessed with her.

Just like it wasn't Blake's fault that he suffered from a mental illness.

"Merry, please," Zack said in a low, rough voice. "I wouldn't ask if it wasn't important."

She stalled, taking a long sip of her sun tea. "I was an only child, and lived next door to the Caruthers when I was growing up. Caroline was my age and we became best friends. I spent more time at the Caruthers' house than I did at my own home, but my parents didn't seem to mind. They were older when they had me, and I think they were a bit overwhelmed by the responsibility of raising a child. And to be honest, I craved being a part of the loud, rambunctious family next door."

Zack reached out to take her hand, and the simple touch helped keep her grounded.

"I had a huge crush on Blake when I was a teenager, but he was two years older and barely noticed me, treating me like another kid sister. Caroline and I both wanted to go to the University of Minnesota and were thrilled to be accepted. We even roomed together. That's when Blake noticed me."

The knot in her stomach tightened painfully. She took a slow breath, staring down at Zack's hand holding hers, so that she didn't have to look him in the eye.

"We began dating, but Blake was different. Moody. He talked to himself and sometimes became violent. One night, he slammed his fist through a glass window and had to be taken to the hospital. His behavior became worse, paranoid and delusional. During his second trip to the hospital he was diagnosed with paranoid schizophrenia."

Zack's fingers tightened on hers, and she forced herself

to meet his gaze. "At first, it wasn't too bad. He was put on medication and seemed to be doing better. But then he stopped taking the medication, claiming he didn't like the side effects. Shortly after that, he attacked me."

"You don't have to tell me anything more," Zack protested, but she ignored him.

"Caroline came to help me and the police took him away. Blake went back on his meds, and then went off them again. Over the next few months, it became a never-ending cycle."

"I'm sorry, Merry," Zack murmured. "I'm so sorry you had to go through that."

"I tried to stay with him. I didn't want to leave Blake just because of his diagnosis. But he wouldn't stay on the meds and without them he was just too impulsive and violent. I had no choice but to break things off."

"You did the right thing."

She shrugged. "After I graduated, I started working as a nurse at one of the hospitals in the Twin Cities, and Blake would always be there, waiting for me at the end of my shift or hanging around my apartment. I moved, but he found me. He attacked me again, so I filed the restraining order. And when that didn't work, I picked up and moved to a different state without telling anyone where I was going."

"And you came here, to Crystal Lake," Zack finished.

She nodded. "I've been here for two years. And I thought I was finally safe. But he must have found me, again, even after all this time."

"I'll keep you safe. You don't have to be afraid of him."

She shook her head, battling a wave of helplessness. "You don't understand, Zack. I'm also worried about you. Blake must have seen you on the patio. He'll assume we're, um, you know." Her cheeks heated and she ducked her head. "He'll see you as a threat. I think it's best if you head back to Madison."

Zack let go of her hand and scowled darkly. She tilted her chin, not caring if she made him mad.

She would rather have him safe. And if that meant being alone until Julie and Derek returned, then that was just fine with her.

5

Zack had to work hard to rein in his temper. Did she really think he was going to leave her here with a crazy man stalking her? Fat chance. What kind of guy did she think he was? As if he cared about whether or not Caruthers came after him? Frankly, he'd welcome the chance to take him down a peg.

Instinctively, he knew Merry wouldn't want to hear that, so he took several deep breaths before turning around to face her.

"I'm staying the weekend, end of discussion. Are you hungry? We could head over to Rose's Café for lunch."

"Don't do this." Her blue eyes pleaded with him. "Don't underestimate Blake."

He narrowed his gaze. "I'm a police officer. I'm more than capable of being your bodyguard. If Blake were smart, he wouldn't underestimate me."

"Maybe we should stay here, keep a low profile."

If he wasn't so angry, he'd be touched by her efforts to protect him. "Actually, I'd like to go to town, see if we can catch a glimpse of his navy blue minivan."

She glanced up at him in surprise. "How did you find out what he's driving?"

"I have connections." He hesitated, wondering if he should tell her everything else he discovered. He didn't want to scare her, yet she needed to understand what she was dealing with. "You need to know Caruthers has done jail time. He has a rather significant criminal record. Drugs, breaking and entering, disorderly conduct."

She didn't look too surprised. "I guess that's more proof he's not taking his medication."

"Please let me take you out to lunch." The moment the sentence left his mouth, he wished he could take it back. He hadn't intended to make it sound like he was asking her out on a date. "I think it would be fun to go into town for a while," he tacked on.

"What about Ace?" she asked, rubbing the dog behind his ears. The lab's head rested on her lap, his eyes gazing up at her adoringly.

"He'll be fine inside for a bit. I'll play with him when we get back."

"All right," she agreed. "But I'll be rather conspicuous in my scrubs."

"You can change if you'd like."

She seemed to consider the idea but then shrugged it off. "I'll wait until later."

He told himself again, to think of Merry like a younger sister, but so far, that tactic wasn't working as well as it should.

"If you're sure." He was anxious to go, partially because he really wanted to see if he could get a glimpse of Blake's van. The sooner he found this guy, the better.

"I'm sure."

Zack put Ace inside the townhouse. "Guard the door, Ace."

The dog thumped his tail, and then stretched out in front of the patio doors as if he'd understood Zack's command.

Merry didn't say much on the short drive into town. He kept his eyes peeled on the road for any sign of a navy blue van with the tag number of 555VRY. They passed a blue van on the highway, and his heart leaped with anticipation, but the plate number didn't match.

Main Street was busy with summer tourists, forcing him to park his truck several blocks down from the café. As they strolled along the sidewalk, he caught sight of the modest Crystal Lake Motel. He paused, scanning the parked cars in the tiny parking lot, figuring if Caruthers was in the area, he had to be staying somewhere.

"Do you see the van?" Merry asked, catching on to what he was doing.

"No." He scowled and reluctantly began walking again. "Could be that he has it down by the public boat launch."

"Or it could be that he's not even here. We don't know for sure that Blake was the guy in the fishing boat."

He didn't bother to argue with her. The boot print beneath the bedroom window, along with the redhead in the fishing boat, was too much of a coincidence to ignore. He held the café door open, the tiny bell jingling to announce their arrival.

"Howdy stranger," Josie greeted him with a broad smile. "It's about time you came back home."

"Just here for the weekend," he pointed out with a grin, even though the word home tugged at his heart. In his mind, Crystal Lake would always be home. Josie was the café owner and self-proclaimed gossip. He knew within minutes the whole town would be buzzing with the news of the prodigal son's return.

"Nice to see you, too, Merry," Josie said with blatant curiosity in her gaze. Zack feared she was already pegging them as a couple. "Find a place to sit, and Darcy will be over shortly."

"No problem." A booth along the row of windows opened up and he nudged Merry in that direction.

"She's going to have us married off in about an hour," Merry muttered half under her breath.

Zack froze for a moment as he was sliding into the booth, and then forced himself to relax. "I could care less what the wagging tongues in Crystal Lake think, but if you're worried, I'll make sure she knows we're just friends."

Merry waved her hand. "It's fine. Hopefully, once you're back in Madison, they'll forget about this and move onto something else."

The thought of leaving Merry here alone while he returned to Madison bothered him. He stared down at the menu, wondering if he could find someone to cover his next few shifts. His boss wouldn't begrudge him the time off, but it was summer and many of the guys had plans.

Everyone except him. Until now.

Grimly, he realized he'd need to find a way to get the time off he needed. There was no way he could leave Crystal Lake. Not yet. Not until he managed to find and arrest Caruthers for violating his restraining order.

He couldn't stand the thought of Merry being hurt again.

MERRY ENJOYED EATING lunch in Rose's Café more than she thought she would. Although she was nonplussed to discover that Josie knew all about how she'd sustained her injuries.

"Are you feeling better, honey?" Josie asked, when she came over to refill their iced teas. "I heard you were injured by one of your patients."

Since Darcy was technically their waitress, Merry figured Josie was trying to get the scoop on details.

"I'm fine, really." Merry didn't want to talk about poor Leonard. For one thing, what happened wasn't his fault. Besides, the government expected healthcare workers to keep patient's information confidential. Obviously, someone at the hospital had talked, but she wasn't about to compound the error.

"Can I get you two anything else?" Josie asked.

"No thanks," Zack responded. She wondered if everyone else in the diner noticed how much he'd stared out the window. She knew he was still searching for the blue van, but now that time had passed since the fishing boat incident, she'd convinced herself that she'd let her imagination run away with her. The possibility of Blake actually looking for her and finding her here in Crystal Lake was extremely remote.

She toyed with her straw, thinking about how much she missed Caroline. Picking up and moving from Minneapolis had been hard, but nothing was as difficult as cutting off all ties with her best friend. And not just Caro, but the entire Caruthers family. She'd loved spending time with the noisy bunch. Had thought about having a big family of her own someday.

But, obviously, that wasn't meant to be. She knew Blake's illness wasn't Caro's fault either, but her friend had inadvertently let key information slip in the past. Blake had found the location to her new apartment in the Twin Cities, just by following Caroline to her place.

Cutting off all ties had been the best thing to do, to stay safe. Caro wouldn't appreciate it if Blake ended up going to jail because of Merry, either.

Her feelings must have been reflected on her face, because Zack reached across the table and took her hand. "What's wrong?"

"Nothing." Subtly, she removed her hand from his, knowing that everyone was already gawking at them. No reason to give them any more to talk about. "Just feeling a little tired, that's all."

"Is your headache back?" he asked with a frown.

"No, I'm fine." The ibuprofen she'd taken earlier had worked wonders. She adjusted the strap of her sling, trying to work the kinks out of her neck. "I guess I find it a little frustrating that I haven't bounced back, yet."

"Now who's doing the underestimating?" he asked in exasperation. "That patient of yours knocked you around pretty badly. I'm amazed you didn't have to stay in the hospital longer than twenty-four hours."

Zack's concern was touching, and she had to remind herself not to read too much into it. She ate the last few bites of her salad, and then pushed her plate away. "I'm ready to leave when you are."

Zack signaled for Darcy to bring their bill. Darcy's flirtatious smile grated on her nerves, but Zack didn't seem to notice. He dug his wallet out and tossed enough money to cover the tab and provide a decent tip. "Let's go."

She didn't say anything when Zack took a detour past the public boat launch, scanning the area for a blue van. And he drove up and down Main Street.

Twice. She was oddly glad that Zack hadn't found any evidence that Blake was here. She even felt a little guilty for making a big deal out of the redhead in the boat.

When they arrived back home, Ace ran around the backyard in circles, obviously excited to see them. True to Zack's word, he tossed a tennis ball for Ace, who threw his whole body into the chase, while she sat in the shade.

She gasped when Ace jumped into the lake, swimming out for the ball, and even more surprised when Zack pulled his phone and his wallet out of his shorts pockets to jump in, too.

It occurred to her that Zack seemed happier now, compared to the last time she'd seen him. She was glad he seemed to be getting over his loss. Although he still hadn't prayed with her before lunch.

Zack's phone beeped and vibrated on the table. She hesitated, and then reached for the phone, thinking she could at least take a message. "Hello?"

There was a long pause on the other end. "I'm sorry, I must have the wrong number," a male voice said.

"No, this is Zack's phone. I'm—a friend of his. He's swimming in the lake right now, but I'd be happy to take a message."

Another pause. "I'm sorry, but did you say swimming?" the man asked, incredulous.

She laughed, realizing that the caller must be a friend of Zack's. Someone who knew him well enough to know that Zack wasn't the average fun-loving guy. "Yes, he's actually swimming. With a black lab named Ace."

"I'm tempted to drive over there, just to see that for myself," the caller said with humor. "You must be Meredith Haines."

The hair on the back of her neck lifted in warning. "Who am I speaking with?" she asked sharply.

"My name is Cole Wallace, and I'm covering Zack's shift today. Have him call me back when he's finished swimming. I've been doing some digging and have a little more information on that Caruthers guy."

She relaxed, realizing that this was clearly Zack's source of information. The fact that Cole was a fellow police officer added to her relief. "All right, but my friends call me Merry, not Meredith. I'll be happy to have Zack call you back."

"Great. Well, it was nice meeting you, Merry."

"Take care, Cole." She pushed the button to end the call, glancing up as Zack approached.

"Too bad you can't swim yet. The water is perfect!" he declared.

She didn't mention that watching him had been just as much fun as swimming herself. She cleared her throat and gestured to his phone. "Your friend Cole called. He mentioned he has information about Blake."

Zack straightened, water dripping off his soggy T-shirt and shorts in tiny waterfalls. "Are you upset with me because I asked Cole to help investigate Caruthers?"

She swallowed hard and shook her head. "No, I'm not upset. But it was a little weird that he knew my name."

Zack dropped into a chair beside her. "I didn't tell him everything," he said softly. "Just enough so he could help me find this guy."

"I know." She forced a smile. "It's just that no one in Crystal Lake knows about my past problems. I guess I was hoping it would stay that way."

"I'm not planning to go around and tell people," Zack said, his gaze serious. "My only goal is to keep you safe."

She stared down at Ace for a minute, wishing desperately that Zack was here because he wanted to be. Because he enjoyed spending time with her. After everything he'd been through, he deserved some relaxation and fun.

Instead, he'd shouldered her problems. And instead of taking well needed time off work, he was having a busman's holiday.

She needed to remember that she was nothing more than another member of the public who he wanted to keep safe.

Her job would be to protect her heart.

ZACK COULD TELL Merry wasn't thrilled with how he'd called Cole for help, but given the same set of circumstances he'd do the same thing again in a heartbeat.

He reached for his phone, but then hesitated when he realized he left his notes inside. He was still sopping wet, although the hot summer sun was beginning to dry him off. He stood and padded over to the patio doors, darting in and out of the kitchen so that he wouldn't get the floor too wet.

Derek had spent a lot of time and muscle refinishing the townhouse that had once suffered from a kitchen fire. He didn't think his new brother-in-law would appreciate water stains on his freshly sanded natural wood floors.

Zack returned to the patio table, wishing Merry wasn't there to listen in on his conversation with Cole. He was anxious to see what his buddy had uncovered, so he didn't want to wait until later.

Besides, the sooner Merry knew exactly what was going on, the better.

He pushed the call back button on his phone and waited for Cole to pick up. "Hello, beautiful."

Zack scowled. "Cole, what are you talking about?"

"Oh, sorry. I thought Merry was calling me back."

Zack had to grit his teeth to prevent himself from snapping his friend's head off. "And just exactly how do you know what she looks like?"

"I pulled up her driver's license photo. She's a cutie. Is she single?"

His fingers tightened on the phone to the point he feared he'd crack the casing. "Knock it off, Cole," he practically growled into the phone. "I thought you had new information for me?"

"Oooh, touchy, aren't you? What's the big deal? You're not planning to break your vow and start dating again, are you?"

Zack could feel Merry's amber eyes boring into him as she listened. He was so not in the mood to have this conversation with Colton, especially not in front of Merry. "Focus, Wallace. I need to know what you found out about Caruthers."

"Oh, I get it," Cole said. "Pretty Merry is sitting right there, isn't she? Okay, here's the deal. A friend of a friend knows a cop in Minneapolis. That cop went over to Caruthers' place and verified the guy isn't home. According to the neighbors, no one has seen him for a few days."

A few days? As in since Tuesday? "Thanks for doing that for me."

"Wait, there's more. Seems Caruthers has to check in with his parole officer once a week, and his last visit was Monday. If he doesn't check in by next Monday, they can arrest him for being in violation of his parole. Of course, he won't do a lot of time, but at least he'll be off the streets for a little while."

"That's excellent news." Zack could barely contain his excitement. "Can I get his parole officer's contact information?"

"Sure." Cole rattled off the name and phone number. "Watch your back, Crain. This guy isn't exactly known to be rational."

"I know. I need one more favor. I need someone to pick up my shift on Monday, too. Can you put the word out for me?"

Cole let out an exaggerated sigh. "I guess I can cover it for you, but you're going to owe me one. Hey, how about this? You introduce me to pretty Merry, I'll willingly wipe the slate clean. How's that for a deal?"

No way, no how. Zack was glad Colton wasn't here to see just how much that idea bothered him. "I'll pay you back, Cole. Tell me what shift you need covered, and if I'm not working I'll take it."

"Hmm, interesting that you seem reluctant to introduce me to your friend. And since I'm a nice guy, I have to think it's because you want her all to yourself."

Okay, enough already. He was finished with this discussion. "Goodbye, Colton." He pushed the end button and forced himself to face Merry as if that embarrassing conversation hadn't just taken place. "I have the name and number of Blake's parole officer. If Caruthers doesn't report in on Monday he risks being arrested for violating his parole."

Merry frowned. "I guess I shouldn't be surprised Blake is on parole. He'll keep ending up in jail if he doesn't take his medication." She tilted her head. "So what else did you discover?"

He glanced down at his scribbled notes, hoping she

hadn't been able to hear Colton's comments. "Cole contacted a friend of a friend who went over to Caruthers' apartment. No one has seen him for a few days."

"I guess that fits our timeline, huh?" Merry's expression was troubled. "I wish I would have gotten a better look at that guy in the fishing boat. For all we know, Blake is visiting his sister or his parents. He might not be here in Crystal Lake at all."

Zack knew she was holding out hope that this would just go away, but he was just as certain that Caruthers was here someplace, watching her.

He stared out over the lake, carefully examining the boats flying back and forth over the water. He was just about to suggest that he go out looking for him, when he caught a glimpse of a man in a blue baseball cap pulled low over his brow.

"You're going to get your wish, because he's out there, right now. Let's go."

Zack rushed down to the boat lift, wishing he'd put the boat in the water earlier. He spun the wheel as rapidly as possible, lowering the frame holding up the speedboat into the water. Merry climbed into the boat and Ace jumped in, too, unwilling to be left behind.

He jammed the key in the ignition and fired up the engine, hoping they weren't too late.

6

Merry held on for dear life as Zack thrust the throttle of the boat forward, zooming over the water. She squinted against the whipping wind, trying to catch a glimpse of the fishing boat. But when she looked at the last place she saw it, the boat was nowhere to be found.

There were lots of other boats on the lake, and Zack had to be careful as he drove, keeping track of the skiers and the tubers.

The boat slowed and Zack glanced over at her. "Do you see him anywhere?"

She shook her head, slowly scanning the water. How was it possible for him to disappear so fast? Then she caught a flash of blue, way over on the opposite side of the lake. "There! Near the public boat launch."

"I see him," Zack muttered grimly. He swung the boat around to give a couple of jet skis a wide berth before heading across the lake.

Merry sat there, her heart racing. She was deeply afraid

of seeing Blake again. The last time he'd attacked her, he'd almost choked her to death.

Her hand crept up to her throat, and for a moment she could still feel the imprint of his strong fingers. Even though she reminded herself that she wasn't alone this time, that Zack was with her, she still didn't want to see him.

Zack slowed the boat as they approached the shore. She clenched her fingers in her lap, trying to remain calm.

"I think that's his boat," Zack said.

She couldn't tell one boat from another but she trusted Zack's keen observation. "Any sign of him?" she asked.

"No, I don't see him." Zack's tone was ripe with frustration. "I'd like to get out and search for him, but I don't want to leave you alone."

She didn't want Zack to leave her alone either, but told herself to stop being a chicken. She reached over and stroked the lab's fur. "I won't be alone. I have Ace."

She could tell Zack wanted to take her up on her offer, but after several long moments he shook his head. "There's plenty of time to track him down. We'll find him."

She couldn't deny feeling a wave of relief. No matter what Zack said, she was worried that Blake would see him as a rival. She'd rather the sheriff's deputies be around to take care of apprehending Blake.

"How's your headache?" Zack asked, as he put the boat in reverse and backed up.

She smiled, for the first time in what seemed like hours. "I'm fine, Zack. Being out on the water is wonderful."

"I'll try to keep a slower pace on the way back," he promised.

"Great, I was hoping you'd take the long way home," she teased.

"Happy to oblige," he responded with a broad smile.

Merry caught her breath at the way his smile lit up his entire face, and she quickly turned in her seat, so that he wouldn't notice her reaction.

She needed to concentrate on relaxing and enjoying the sunshine, not imagining what it would be like to be with Zack as more than a friend.

ZACK FELT AMAZINGLY CONTENT, appreciating the sense of calmness that surrounded him when he was out on the water. He was annoyed that he hadn't been able to catch up with Caruthers but he did get the number off the boat's hull and could use that to find out who rented it.

He was confident he'd have the guy behind bars, soon.

Per Merry's request, he took the long way back to their pier, cruising along the edge of the lake. He saw several new houses along the shoreline that he didn't remember seeing before, as well as a few properties that were for sale, including a tiny cottage almost surrounded by trees not far from his sister's place. There were still a few empty lots that were also for sale, and it occurred to him that maybe he should invest in one, just in case.

He mentally rolled his eyes at his foolish thought. In case of what? He'd made a decision to move away from Crystal Lake, so there was no reason at all to consider buying a lot. What was wrong with him, today? He needed to remember that this was just a nice mini-vacation, nothing more.

Glancing over he saw Merry was relaxed in her seat, her face tipped into the wind while she rested her hand on Ace's head, idly scratching him behind the ears. He was struck once again by her beauty, and was forced to silently admit that he didn't want her to meet his buddy Cole. Because he wanted her for himself?

Yes. No. Maybe.

She was what was wrong with him today. Ever since he'd begun to spend time with Merry, his traitorous thoughts kept wondering what it would be like to spend time with her more often. Like on a date. Ridiculous to consider such foolishness. For one thing, she was a devout Christian, and no matter what she said, he knew that God had given up on him. Besides, she deserved a family of her own and that was the one thing he knew he couldn't do. No way, no how.

Tearing his gaze away from Merry, he glanced around at the other boaters, making sure that Caruthers hadn't returned. There was no sign of the fishing boat, and while he knew he should get back to his sister's place so he could start making phone calls, he didn't want to get off the lake just yet.

After a good forty-five minutes, he turned the speedboat back toward the pier. They hadn't brought any sunscreen and he was concerned Merry's pale skin would burn.

As he pulled up alongside the pier, Merry stood and reached over to grasp the side of the lift, helping to guide the boat into position. She acted like an experienced boat rider, and he wondered if that was because she'd gone out with Julie several times.

"Thanks Zack," she murmured as he finagled the boat into place. "That was a nice ride, at least on the way back."

"You're welcome." He needed to get away from her. Fast. Before he did something stupid like try to kiss her. "I have to run into town, would you mind heading inside with Ace while I'm gone? And lock the doors, too."

She frowned but then shrugged. "I guess I can do that. I wouldn't mind resting again for a little bit. Even though I haven't done anything all day, I'm still exhausted."

"You need to listen to what your body is trying to tell you," he said, taking her arm to help her get out of the boat, and then following her up the grassy embankment to return to the house. "How about I stop at the store and pick up something for dinner? I wouldn't mind grilling out tonight."

Merry kept her eyes downcast, and her cheeks were pink, no doubt from the sun. "Sure, that's fine. I'll raid Julie's garden and make salads."

He wouldn't say no to fresh veggies, but hoped that he hadn't made the invitation to share dinner sound like anything other than what it was, friends sharing a meal. It seemed stupid for each of them to make their own separate dinners.

"See you later," he said casually, as Merry went inside his sister's place, taking Ace with her. He waited until he heard the door lock click into place before he crossed over to his side of the townhouse. A little distance from Merry was exactly what he needed right now. He went into the bedroom and rifled through his duffel bag to find his badge and his gun before heading back out to the main living area. Grabbing his truck keys from the counter, he headed out front to where he'd left his pickup parked on the road.

The drive into town, for the second time that day, didn't take long. He wanted to stop at the rental place first, to see if he could convince the owner to let him know who'd taken out the fishing boat. Granted, he had his badge and his weapon but he clearly wasn't wearing his uniform, and anyone with half a brain would know he wasn't on duty.

He didn't recognize the young man behind the counter of Boats Are Us, so he pulled out his badge and glanced at the name tag pinned to the man's shirt. "Hi, Dave, I'm a cop, and I need to know who rented a fishing boat earlier today."

Dave pushed his glasses up his nose as he glanced at the badge, and then frowned. "We rent a lot of boats, Officer. I couldn't begin to tell you who rented what."

Zack nodded. "I have the number off the hull." He scribbled the number on a scrap piece of paper and slid it across the counter. "Do me a favor and check your files, okay?"

Dave hesitated, as if he thought he was doing something wrong. "Maybe I should call my boss."

Zack shrugged. "You can do that. I can also call my friends at the Hope County Sheriff's Department to rush things along, as well. What's the big deal? It's just a name, right?"

"I guess," Dave mumbled. He picked up the number and went over to the computer system. He tapped on the keys, searching for the information. "Here it is. The guy's name is Calvin Reynolds, and he rented the boat for a week."

What? Zack scowled and wished he could see the computer screen for himself. "Are you sure? Check again."

"I'm sure. It's right here." Dave jabbed his finger on the computer screen.

Zack couldn't believe it. Was it possible he'd gotten the number wrong? "Okay, try this then. Search for the name Blake Caruthers."

This time it took Dave much longer, and at one point Zack actually spelled out the last name, in case Dave had it misspelled.

"Nope, don't have anyone in the system by that name," Dave said with a sigh. "Sorry."

Zack stared at him, trying to figure out if he was really wrong or if Dave was actually covering for Blake by lying to him. He didn't want to believe he could be that paranoid, so he thanked Dave and turned away.

Then he swung back. "Tell me something, that first name you mentioned, Calvin Reynolds. You said he paid for a week. What day did he rent the boat?"

Dave went back to tapping on the computer keyboard. "Tuesday morning."

Coincidence? Zack wasn't about to leave any stone unturned. "How did he pay, with a credit card?"

"Actually he paid cash, but we require a credit card number on file in case there's any damage to the property."

Was Caruthers smart enough to get a fake credit card and driver's license? He wasn't sure. Maybe Zack was the one being paranoid. "Did you happen to catch what type of vehicle he was driving?" Zack asked.

"No. I wasn't here when he rented the boat."

"I see." Zack knew he couldn't count on Dave to describe the guy, then, either. "One last thing. Any chance you know the address that goes along with the credit card? Any chance it's from out of state? Say, Minnesota?"

Dave folded his arms over his chest. "Look, Officer, I tried to help you, but I can't run the credit card address for you. I don't even know how, even if I wanted to. If you need that information, then you may as well call your deputy friends."

Zack shrugged. "All right, I'll do that. Thanks for your help."

He turned and left the boat rental, trying to understand this latest clue. Or lack of a clue. Somehow, he just couldn't buy the idea that a red-haired guy who looked like Caruthers just happened to rent a boat for the week. Reynolds had to be Caruthers.

The scary part was that even with his psych history,

Caruthers was going well out of his way to cover his tracks. As if he had more on his mind than simply scaring Merry or just trying to talk to her.

But how could Zack prove it? He went back outside and, once again, drove up and down Main Street to look for the blue van. If he found that, he'd know for sure that Reynolds and Caruthers were one and the same.

He drove into the motel parking lot, but as before, there was no sign of the blue van. He drummed his fingers on the top of the steering wheel, wondering how many other places there were to stay in Hope County? Probably way more than he wanted to know.

It suddenly hit him that he was looking for a van, and there was a campground located not too far outside the Crystal Lake city limits. Why hadn't he thought of a campground? Caruthers could be sleeping in the back of his van or in a tent. Cheap and with easy access in and out of the city.

Zack backed out of the motel parking lot, turned around, and then headed for the highway, a keen sense of anticipation rushing through his system. This was a good lead and, with any luck, he'd have proof Caruthers not only violated his restraining order but also committed identity theft.

He dialed Cole's number as he drove. "Hey, I need you to run a check on another name for me."

Colton sighed. "You're just full of favors today, aren't you? All right, what do you have?"

Zack quickly filled him in on the boat chase, and the information he'd uncovered from the Boats Are Us rental agency. "I really think Caruthers is using this fake name, Calvin Reynolds. See if you can find out if he has any friends or known associates by that name."

"Okay, but explain why you can't do your own legwork on this?" Cole asked. "I'm the one working your shift, while you're slacking off on your boat."

"I would, but I'm heading over to the Hope County Campground. I've been driving all around town and haven't seen that van, but never considered he might be using a tent to camp out."

"Good point," Cole muttered. "All right, give me some time with this and I'll get back to you."

"Thanks, Cole."

Zack ended the call, trying not to be too disappointed. After all, Cole was working his shift. He couldn't complain about the fact that Cole had put his job first and Zack's request for information second.

The campground was only seven miles down the highway, and he slowed his truck and turned carefully onto the gravel driveway. The conditions were typical of any other campground—a building housing bathrooms and showers, with several paths winding around the area, providing many opportunities to pitch a tent or park a camper.

Zack took his time, driving super slow and checking out the area. There were dozens of campsites and he knew this might take a while. He was tempted to call Merry to let her know but held back, just in case she was sleeping. And he needed to pick up something to cook her for dinner.

Enough, already. He shook his head as if he could dislodge his wayward brain cells. He needed to concentrate on finding Caruthers rather than constantly thinking about Merry. He was helping to keep her safe, nothing more. As soon as he'd found the guy and arrested him, he'd head back to Madison, where he belonged.

The sooner, the better.

Merry stretched out on her bed, her eyelids feeling incredibly heavy. How she could feel so tired, she had no idea. She hadn't done anything even remotely physical. She hated to admit how much the concussion she'd sustained had affected her.

Ace settled down on the floor beside her bed, his tail thumping reassuringly against the floor. "Good boy," she murmured. Having Ace around helped her feel grounded and safe. Slowly, she relaxed, and eventually felt herself drift off to sleep.

Ace's barking broke through her nightmare, moments before Blake was going to kill her. She awoke with a start, her heart pounding in her chest. What was wrong? Based on the blue lights of Julie's alarm clock, almost two hours had passed.

She rolled out of bed, wincing as she moved her arm without the sling to help remind her to keep it still. She hurried out to the main living area, where Ace's barks had turned into a low, menacing growl.

"Ace? What's wrong? Did you see a squirrel?" Ace was known to take all threats, even small furry ones, seriously. He'd scared her more than once with his ferocious barking, only to discover a rabbit had ventured too close to the patio.

As she approached the kitchen area, she caught a glimpse of a face pressed against the small window above the sink.

For a moment she could only stare in horror but then she let out an ear-shattering scream.

7

Zack pulled in front of the townhouse and was walking up to the front door when he heard Merry scream. His heart lodged in his throat and he leaped up on the front porch and yanked at the door, belatedly remembering he'd locked it on his way out.

"Merry!" He shouted, as he fumbled for his keys. "It's Zack! I'm here!"

Ace's barking joined the melee, and Zack finally found the key and twisted it in the lock. He dashed inside, following the sounds to the kitchen area.

She stood, still wearing her badly wrinkled scrubs, shaking as she pointed to the window. "It was—right—there!" she stuttered.

He couldn't stop himself from wrapping his arms around her, to try and settle her down. "What was there? Did you see something?"

"A face. In the kitchen window."

Caruthers had been here? Zack thought fast, going through the options. Had Caruthers escaped down to the lake or around to the front where he may have left a car? "Stay here with Ace and lock the doors. I'll be right back."

Leaving Merry wasn't easy, but there wasn't a moment to lose. He hadn't found the blue van at the campsite, though there were plenty of tents without vehicles that could have belonged to Caruthers. He'd hated to come back without the evidence he needed. But now he had a chance.

Zack dashed through the patio door, down to the lake. He figured that since he hadn't seen any sign of the blue van when he'd returned home, Caruthers must have used the fishing boat again. But he didn't see any sign of it. How much time had passed since Merry saw the face in the window? Five minutes? Less?

He scanned the area, looking for anything remotely suspicious. But there was nothing. No fishing boat. No redhead in a baseball cap.

Could he have missed him out front? He wasn't sure how, but decided to double check. He ran around the side of the house back to the street. In the distance, he could hear the sound of an engine.

He didn't hesitate, but jumped into his truck. He didn't see anything to the east, so he grabbed his sunglasses to cut the glare and drove west, directly into the setting sun, down the road toward the highway that lead away from town.

Was that Caruthers up ahead? Zack could just barely make out a dark colored vehicle way off in the distance, but he couldn't be sure that it was a van verses any other SUV type of vehicle. Thankfully, his truck had a big engine, and he floored the accelerator in an attempt to gain some ground.

But after he came over the crest of a hill, there was nothing in front of him on the highway.

He slammed his fist on the steering wheel, venting his

frustration. He was a better cop than this. How could he have lost him? Had Caruthers gotten off on one of the side streets? And if so, which one?

Slowing down at each intersection, and there really weren't that many, he tried to get a glimpse of the dark colored vehicle. There were a few other cars, but none resembling a blue van.

Every instinct he possessed told him to keep searching, but the memory of how Merry had looked, so shattered and alone, convinced him to turn around and go back.

Was it possible she imagined the whole thing? No, he heard the car engine and Ace had been barking. Caruthers had some nerve, showing up at the townhouse in broad daylight.

And then it hit him. His truck hadn't been parked outside. Had Caruthers noticed that small detail and decided to make an attempt at getting to Merry? Or had Caruthers followed him? Had Merry's former boyfriend caught a glimpse of Zack leaving alone and decided to make his move?

At this point, anything was possible. Caruthers could have seen him in town, for all he knew. And while Zack had been checking out the campground, Caruthers had gone back to the townhouse.

Zack pulled up in front of his sister's place, grimly realizing he couldn't afford to make the mistake of leaving Merry home alone, again.

He'd have to stick to her like glue, no matter how difficult that was for him. Her safety was more important than his reluctant attraction.

He'd just have to find a way to deal with it.

MERRY BOWED her head and prayed for strength and guidance, for herself and for Zack. Feeling calmer after she'd locked all the doors, she sat on the edge of the sofa, holding Ace close to her side. She tried to remember any details from the brief glimpse of the face at the window, but already her memory was a bit fuzzy.

Zack returned about twenty minutes later, once again using his key to come in the front door. By the dejected set of his shoulders, she guessed he hadn't caught up with Blake. If the face at the window even belonged to him. Was it possible she had two stalkers in one lifetime? She sincerely hoped not.

"I'm sorry, Merry," Zack said, rubbing the back of his neck. "Somehow I lost him."

She forced a smile. "It's okay, I'm just glad Ace was here with me. His barking woke me up from a sound sleep." She decided not to mention the nightmare. After all, there was nothing Zack could do about it.

He dropped into a chair at the kitchen table. "You woke up when you heard Ace barking? And then what, you came out into the kitchen?"

She nodded. "Sometimes Ace barks at chipmunks, squirrels, or other dogs, so I didn't really think too much about it. But when I came into the kitchen he was growling, and that's when I looked up and saw the face. His hands were cupped around his forehead and cheeks, as if to cut out the glare from the sunlight so he could see inside better."

"And that's when you screamed?" Zack asked.

She felt her cheeks flush with embarrassment. "It all happened so fast, I think he may have disappeared already by that time, but I can't say for sure. I normally don't lose control like that."

"You don't have to apologize. You have every right to scream when you find someone peeking into your window." Zack sighed and shook his head. "I'm the one who's failed you. He was so close. I should have been able to catch up with him."

She hated the way he was beating himself up over this, and wished he'd share his burdens with God.

"Zack, if you were on duty you would have had backup for assistance. You can't be everywhere at one time. Did you find out who rented the fishing boat?"

He grimaced. "Another dead end. But I still need to follow up with Cole to see what he found out. And I picked up hamburgers and brats for dinner. Hope that's okay."

"It's perfect. I'll go outside and pick some veggies out of the garden."

Zack shot to his feet. "Wait. I need to look around, just in case he left another footprint or some other clue. Stay here with Ace for just a little while longer, okay?"

She nodded and didn't protest when he went back outside through the patio door. After another ten minutes, he returned and held the door open as an invitation to come outside. "I didn't find anything, but that's probably not surprising. You had the shades pulled in the bedroom, so I'm guessing he didn't bother to try to look through those windows. And of course, I didn't find anything out here on the concrete patio."

Was it possible Zack didn't really believe her? No, after all, he'd taken off looking for Blake, going as far as to try and follow him in the truck. Surely Zack believed in her.

Just as a precaution, she kept Ace next to her as she worked in the garden. While picking vegetables, she pulled a few weeds and made a mental note to water later tonight once the sun went down. Julie had encouraged her to eat the vegetables in the garden so they wouldn't go bad in the time she and Derek were gone.

Merry gathered cucumbers, lettuce, peppers, onions and tomatoes using the hem of her scrub top to hold everything together. Her shoulder was still sore, but she didn't want to put the sling on just yet.

"Looks good," Zack commented, as he held the patio door open for her. As soon as she disappeared inside, he went back to cleaning up the grill.

The domesticated scene seemed a bit surreal. If she didn't know better, she'd think Zack planned on settling down again someday.

But she didn't dare get her hopes up. Even if he did ask her out, which she could scarcely imagine, he wasn't a Christian. So there was no point in even considering getting involved with him.

Merry shook off the depressing thought and concentrated on washing the veggies and cutting them up for salads. She could hear Zack whistling as he grilled the brats and burgers, and she wondered if he realized how lighthearted he sounded. Despite everything with Blake, he seemed to be more relaxed and content than ever.

She went into the bedroom, anxious to change out of her scrubs that were now stained with sweat and soil from being out in the garden. Washing up at the bathroom sink wasn't too difficult, but when it came to pulling on a T-shirt to wear with her Capri jeans, a sharp pain zinged down her arm.

Struggling with the fabric and her limited range of motion wasn't easy, but eventually she managed, whimpering only a little when she finally got her injured arm through the opening.

She took several deep breaths, willing the pain to subside. Reluctantly, she pulled the sling back on. By the time she returned to the kitchen she was surprised to find that Zack had dinner ready. He'd taken the salads outside and had set out plates and silverware on the patio table. In the center was a large platter full of meat, buns and condiments, including several choices of salad dressing.

"Wow," she managed as she pulled out a chair to sit down. "I'm impressed."

Zack took the seat to her right, the umbrella helping to shade them from the worst of the setting sun. He glanced at her, and waited.

It took her a minute to realize he was giving her time to pray. Pleased, she bowed her head and spoke out loud, hoping to find the words that may get through to him.

"Dear Lord, we thank You for this bountiful meal we're about to eat. We also ask that You give us strength and wisdom to get to the bottom of the mystery surrounding us. And lastly, we ask for You to ease the ache in our hearts for the loved ones we've lost, Amen."

She glanced over at Zack to find him staring down at his empty plate, his hands folded loosely in his lap. Was it possible he'd been praying, too? She reminded herself not to get her hopes up.

"Did you really lose someone close to you? Or was that last part just for me?" Zack asked in a low voice.

Her heart ached for him. "I did. My parents passed away when I was in college. My father died of a heart attack. My mother died shortly afterwards and no one could figure out why. I always figured she died of a broken heart."

"If you could die of a broken heart, I'd be dead by now," Zack muttered. "Cancer is a horrible disease."

She wanted badly to reach out and hug him, but feared he'd reject the slightest bit of comfort. "I know it is, and I know that you've suffered greatly. But try to remember that as hard as it is for you, I truly believe your wife and daughter are in a much better place with God."

"I wish I could know that for sure," Zack said.

"You'll just have to find a way to believe God's word," she said. "I've worked in the ER for several years now, and I've had two different patients tell me that they saw a bright light as we were resuscitating them. I guess that's the closest thing to proof that I can give you."

"A patient really told you that?"

She nodded. "Yes, as recently as a few months ago. One of our church members was in a terrible car crash last year, and the paramedics brought him in doing CPR the entire time. Afterward, he told me that he wasn't afraid to die because he saw the light and knew that heaven would be there for him when it was his time."

Zack stared at her for a long minute before he gave a brief nod. "I always thought those were just stories."

"Many stories have a kernel of truth to them, and I promise you, this one is absolutely true. If you tried to tell Mr. Graybar that he was imagining things, he'd be sure to set you straight." She picked up her fork and dug into her salad.

Zack picked up the platter and held it out for her, before choosing both a hamburger and a brat for himself. As they ate, the conversation veered toward less intense subjects than everlasting life.

"I went through the campground off Hwy ZZ, to see if I could find Caruthers blue van," Zack said between bites.

"Little did I know that he'd end up back here, peeping into the kitchen window."

She was thrilled that he believed her. "I'm thankful Ace was there to sound the alarm."

At the sound of his name, the dog jumped up and padded over. "No begging," she said in a stern voice. Ace whirled around and plopped back down on the ground near her feet.

"He's very well trained," Zack said, glancing down at the dog. "I know you're just watching him for Julie and Derek, but I can tell you already love him. You should consider getting a dog of your own."

"I can't have pets in my apartment complex," she reminded him. "But I wouldn't mind a dog like Ace. He's been great company."

"I was thinking I might look for a dog, too."

"Really?" She was surprised to hear that. "You must live somewhere that allows pets."

He shrugged and nodded. "Yeah, I live in the upper level of a duplex. There's a nice couple living below me. I do all the heavy work, like snow-blowing, mowing, minor repairs, and they give me a nice cut on my rent. I don't think they'd mind if I owned a dog."

Merry thought that Julie would be thrilled to know Zack wouldn't be living all alone. "Would you have time to train him?"

"I guess I'd have to make the time, but I don't think it would be that difficult."

"I wouldn't have a clue where to start. I'd have to find someone to train my dog for me." Merry finished her salad and started on her burger, discovering that eating a sandwich with one hand wasn't as easy as it sounded. "This is delicious, Zack. Thanks so much."

"It's the least I can do." He seemed to avoid her gaze and she figured he was trying to keep things casual so she wouldn't misinterpret this as some sort of date.

A fact she'd be wise to remember.

ZACK COULDN'T SEEM to pry Merry's story out of his mind. Of course after Suzanne and Amelia had died, the pastor of the church had tried to tell him that they were up in heaven, but he hadn't been able to believe it. Hadn't been able to believe in a God who would take two innocent lives away from him.

But now, for some reason he wanted to believe Amelia and Suz were really were up there. In a place that was bright and warm. Where they would forever be safe from harm. Close to God.

Merry started cleaning up the dishes, carrying things into the house a little at a time. He stood to help her, but then his phone rang. He eagerly picked up the call. "Hey Cole, do you have more information?"

"Yeah, I've been running the Calvin Reynolds name and guess what? There is a guy by that name living in the Twin Cities and he's done some jail time too, at the same facility as that Caruthers dude."

"I knew it!" Zack jumped to his feet, too excited to sit still. "This has to be the same guy. He's using his friend's identity to cover his tracks."

"It's a strong theory, that's for sure," Cole agreed. "And a bit concerning. What in the world is he planning?"

Good question. "I don't know but he's not going to get to

her. Now that I'm onto him, I'll find a way to bring him down."

"Hey, I believe you. How's pretty Merry holding up?"

Zack ground his molars together for a brief moment, fighting the surge of temper. "She's fine. A little on edge, which is completely understandable, but otherwise fine."

"So, still not willing to introduce us, huh?"

Zack ignored the taunt, knowing that Cole was only trying to get under his skin. "No point. She's too good for the likes of you."

"Hey, that means she's too good for you, too."

Zack rolled his eyes. "Back to Reynolds, any chance you can send someone to pick him up? Maybe ask him a few questions?"

"On what grounds?"

"Identity theft. Tell him that you discovered someone's been charging up his credit card and that you're worried about his credit rating."

"I doubt Reynolds cares one bit about his credit rating, but I might be able to use the identity theft angle." Cole sighed. "You're going to owe me big time for all these favors, you know. Although, considering you haven't asked for anything in over two years, I'm still reeling from shock."

Zack had done plenty of favors for Cole, but he knew that doing a side investigation like this was a much bigger deal than covering a few shifts. "I know, and I really appreciate it."

"All right, I'll let you know what happens."

"Thanks." Zack disconnected from the call and stuffed the phone in his back pocket. He gathered up what was left of the dishes and carried them inside.

He was in the process of setting the stack on the counter just moments before Merry turned around and plowed into him. She was knocked off balance and he lightly grasped her shoulders to steady her.

"Are you okay?" he asked.

"Sorry, I'm a klutz." Her free hand was on his chest and for several long moments he gazed into her amber eyes.

There was absolutely no rational reason or viable excuse for what he did next. His vow of remaining emotionally distant from Merry, keeping her at arm's length, evaporated in a puff of smoke.

Instead, he drew her closer, lowered his head and kissed her.

8

Merry was startled by Zack's unexpected kiss, but only for a second. He tasted wonderful, and her fingers curled in the fabric of his T-shirt to hold herself steady as she opened for him.

Zack's kiss was tender yet demanding at the same time. She reveled in the embrace, unable to remember the last time she'd kissed a man. Certainly not since well before she'd moved to Crystal Lake.

But the heated embrace was all too brief. Zack abruptly lifted his head, pulled away and stepped back. She reluctantly released her grip on his shirt and leaned against the counter for support.

"I shouldn't have done that," Zack said in a low, gravely tone. His blue eyes clearly reflected his regret. "I'm sorry. You deserve..." He shook his head. "More. I don't have anything to give you."

She wanted to protest, but before she could get the words out, Zack turned and left, shutting the patio door behind him.

For several long moments she stood there, trying to

gather her scattered thoughts. She'd reveled in Zack's kiss. Had secretly hoped he'd kiss her ever since the first night she met him. And she hadn't been disappointed.

But clearly Zack did not feel the same way. Granted, he'd initiated the kiss but considered it a momentary lapse in judgment. Something that he obviously had no intention of allowing to happen again.

She took a deep breath and turned back to the counter full of dirty dishes. Merry didn't mind washing them. Considering Zack had purchased and made the meal, it was the least she could do. Washing them one handed wasn't easy, and after a few minutes, she shucked out of the stupid sling and finished the dishes, leaving them in the sink to air dry.

There was no sign of Zack outside, so she let Ace out for one last doggy bathroom break, before calling him back in. She tried not to feel hurt that he was avoiding her.

The truth hurts, Merry. Suck it up.

Thanks to her two naps, she wasn't the least bit sleepy. She took her Bible and settled in the corner of the sofa to read some of her favorite Psalms to ease her troubled soul.

Somehow, she just knew that if she could help Zack find his way back to his faith, he'd be able to let himself find love and happiness again.

But even with that miracle, there was no guarantee that his future would ever include her.

MERRY WOKE up to Ace whining in her ear. The dog was

better than any alarm clock she'd ever owned, she thought wryly as she staggered out of bed.

"Alright, I'm coming." Why she persisted in talking to the dog she had no idea. The thought of possibly getting a dog was becoming more appealing by the day. She ignored the constant ache in her shoulder as she headed out to the living area to where Ace was already waiting rather impatiently near the patio door.

She unlocked and opened the door. Ace bounded outside, energy radiating from every pore. There was no sign of Zack, not that she was terribly surprised. She didn't anticipate any offers to cook breakfast, either.

Maybe he hadn't liked kissing her. After all, she was out of practice. No one had ever said she was good at kissing even when she had been in the dating scene. She gathered cold cereal and yogurt for breakfast and sat at the kitchen table where she could watch Ace outside.

For some odd reason, she felt incredibly lonely. Ridiculous since she'd been eating breakfast alone for years. Why did she suddenly miss Zack's presence now? A few shared meals did not make a relationship.

She shook her head at her foolishness. By the time she'd finished her breakfast, Ace was back at the door, wagging his tail as if telling her he wanted to come in.

She opened the door, sweeping her gaze over the lake. There was no sign of the fishing boat this morning, which she chose to believe was a positive sign.

"Good dog," she murmured, scratching him behind the ears. She was tempted to walk over and offer Zack the ability to play with Ace, but then realized that was just an excuse.

She wanted to see Zack. To spend time with him.

Pathetic enough to take whatever scraps of companionship he was willing to share.

Enough, she told herself firmly. Zack was right about one thing, she did deserve more than he was willing to give. Hadn't she dreamed of having a large family of her own? No point in even thinking Zack would be willing to be a part of her future.

She showered and spent far too long trying to brush and dry her hair, hampered by her cracked collarbone. Wielding the blow dryer wasn't easy, and she gave up after a few minutes. She left her hair down, and then struggled to get dressed.

Her shoulder was incredibly sore by the time she was ready, so she popped some ibuprofen, washing it down with sun tea. Glancing at the clock, she realized she'd need to leave soon if she was going to make it on time for choir practice.

Should she tell Zack where she was going? She was tempted not to disturb him, but then again, she didn't want him to worry if he happened to discover she was gone.

She decided against carrying a purse, and took Ace with her as she went out the patio door to Zack's side of the townhouse. She felt a little foolish knocking on the doorframe. "Zack?" she called through the screen door. "I'm heading out to choir practice, so I'm leaving Ace with you."

Zack crossed over to glare at her. "I don't think it's smart for you to go off on your own."

"Well, good morning to you, too." She didn't bother to hide her irritation. "I slept well, thanks for asking."

He sighed and rubbed the back of his neck. "Look, I'm sorry, but I wasn't expecting you to announce that you're leaving. Give me a few minutes to get ready and I'll give you a lift."

It was on the tip of her tongue to refuse, but there was a part of her that knew Zack would only argue until he got his way. "Okay, but please hurry. I don't want to be late."

"Come inside for a minute." He opened the door for her and Ace.

True to his word, Zack didn't make her wait long. He came out of the bathroom, the scent of his aftershave reminding her of their kiss.

She averted her gaze, hoping her blush wasn't too noticeable. With any luck, singing hymns at church would help put everything in perspective.

Because, clearly, she needed all the help she could get.

ZACK TRIED NOT to take his foul mood out on Merry. It certainly wasn't her fault that he'd been unable to sleep.

He'd kissed her, so how could he complain when she kissed him back?

She'd been in his mind before he finally fell asleep and was the first person he'd thought about when he woke up. Man, he had it bad. And as much as he tried to tell himself that he was just worried about Caruthers, he couldn't bring himself to keep lying to himself.

He liked Merry. He enjoyed being with her, even doing nothing more than sitting together on the patio watching the boaters on the lake. And he'd missed her in the measly twelve hours they'd been apart.

Get a grip, he told himself firmly. All morning he'd been trying to keep Suzanne and Amelia in the forefront of his mind, but to no avail. He forced himself to concentrate on the road, keeping a keen eye out for a blue van.

"I'm assuming choir practice is at the church?"

"Yes. I'll be there for an hour and a half, if you want to go home and come back later."

She hadn't looked him directly in the eye since snapping at him, and he wondered if she'd thought about that bone-melting kiss as much as he had. Or was that just wishful thinking on his part?

"I'll stay." The thought of sitting in the church made him antsy, but what else could he do? He'd promised himself not to leave her alone again. And the fact that she'd be with a bunch of old people singing in a church choir didn't count as adequate protection, at least not in his book. So he'd sit in the back of the church and wait for her to finish.

Thankfully, he had his smart phone to help keep him busy.

He caught sight of the white church steeple between a break in the trees. The ride from Julie's place didn't take long, and soon he was pulling into the church parking lot adjacent to the building that looked achingly familiar.

Well over two years had passed since he'd crossed the threshold, since the day of Suzanne's funeral. For a moment his hands went damp and droplets of sweat beaded along his temple. He hadn't anticipated this visceral of a reaction to being here again. It was just a structure. Nothing more. No reason to flip out or anything.

"Thanks," Merry murmured as she moved to get out of the passenger seat. The sound of her voice helped ground him, and he put his hand out to prevent her from leaving.

"Wait for me." He quickly pushed open the driver's side door and climbed out. He rounded the truck, sweeping his gaze over the parking lot to make sure he hadn't missed the blue van.

He opened Merry's door for her, and helped her out. He followed as she headed inside.

The interior of the church was nice and cool, a welcome relief from the hot sun outside. He slid into one of the pews in the back, positioning himself where he could keep an eye on the doorway.

"Merry! We weren't sure you were going to make it," one of the elderly women greeted her. "How are you feeling, dear?"

"I'm fine, and why wouldn't I be here? A cracked collarbone wouldn't keep me from singing."

Just as he suspected, the choir was made up of mostly older adults, although he frowned when he noticed a younger man, maybe a few years older than him, giving Merry a hug. Who was that guy? Hadn't she said she wasn't seeing anyone?

Zack subtly moved up a few pews, straining to hear the guy's name.

"Hi Daniel, nice to see you," Merry said, returning the hug. Daniel wasn't very tall, just a couple inches taller than Merry, but he was clean-cut with sandy brown hair and sporting a well-trimmed goatee.

Zack rubbed his freshly shaved cheek, wondering if Merry liked men with facial hair. His beard always itched, but if that was what she wanted...

He stopped himself, mentally smacking his forehead. Losing it. He was clearly losing it.

He took his phone out and searched his e-mail for any further news from Cole, trying to ignore the group milling about the piano at the front of the church. Daniel was probably exactly what Merry needed. A nice guy who'd give her the family she so clearly wanted. Not that she'd said anything, but the way her eyes had glowed as she talked about growing up next to the Caruthers had clued him in.

When the choir began to sing, he found himself arrested by the sweet merging of voices. He could distinguish Merry's voice clearly above the others and was secretly surprised at the beautiful sound.

For a moment the music washed over him, bringing back a rush of memories, and not all of them bad. He and his family had gone to church regularly. Suz hadn't been able to carry a tune, but Amelia had been a part of the children's choir, dressed as an angel during the annual Christmas pageant, her wings hanging crooked because she'd tripped and fallen on the way up the aisle.

Tears burned behind his eyes, and he held them off with an effort.

He missed them so much. But he couldn't help thinking about what Merry had said about his family being up in heaven. For the first time since burying them, he lifted his eyes to the top of the church as if seeking the answer to his unspoken question. Was there really a God? Were his wife and daughter in a much better place now? He noticed the cross hanging above the altar and a strange sense of peace washed over him.

Of course Suzanne and Amelia were up in heaven. Why wouldn't they be? They'd both been good Christians and had believed in God. Had he been selfish to wallow in their passing?

Probably. He'd wanted them to stay here with him.

The choir finished their song, discussed things for a few minutes, and then moved on to the next one. This hymn was an upbeat song meant to lift the spirits of the churchgoers, and he found himself tapping his foot to the beat.

Maybe it wasn't quite the country western songs he tended to prefer, but for whatever reason, he enjoyed the songs just the same.

He stared at his phone, wishing Cole would come up with something, anything to give him a clue as to where he could find Caruthers. Surely Reynolds would spill something useful.

And then it hit him. They were looking for the blue van that was registered to Caruthers. Maybe they should be looking for the vehicle that Reynolds normally drove? After all, Caruthers had a credit card and an ID belonging to the guy. Why not trade vehicles too?

Heart racing with excitement, he sent a quick text message to Cole. *What does Reynolds drive? Need make model and tag# thx.*

Maybe now they could get somewhere. Too bad he hadn't considered this earlier. All this time he'd been chasing after a blue van when in reality he had no clue what Caruthers might be driving.

Ten agonizing minutes later, Cole returned his message. *Ten year old black Jeep Cherokee 555-CVB.*

A black Jeep fit with the dark vehicle he'd followed last evening and was strong enough to tow a fishing boat. Armed with this new information, he itched to get back into town, to swing past the Crystal Lake Motel and run through the campground again.

Any luck getting Reynolds to talk?

He hasn't been home yet.

Zack scowled at the message, his fingers flying over the keys. *Keep trying.*

He realized the music had stopped and glanced up to see what was happening. The members of the choir seemed to be taking a break, all except for Merry and that Daniel guy who were deep in conversation.

Zack shot out of the pew and headed up the aisle before he realized what he was doing. "Merry? Do you have a minute?"

She glanced at him in surprise, and smiled. "Sure, excuse me, Daniel."

He slowed to a stop, feeling a bit foolish for interrupting them. She walked toward him, her amber eyes quizzical. "What's up?"

Zack cleared his throat. "I'm sorry to interrupt you, but I need to ask if you can recall seeing a black Jeep hanging around. Maybe in those few days before you were injured at work?"

"A black Jeep?" She frowned and shook her head. "Sorry, but that doesn't ring a bell. Why?"

"We've been looking for a blue van, but it's entirely possible Caruthers is driving a black Jeep instead."

She nodded slowly. "Okay, that's good to know."

"So who's the guy? Daniel?" he asked, striving for a casual tone. "He seems to like you."

For a moment Merry looked flustered. "Oh, no. He's just a friend. He's one of the physical therapists at the hospital."

"No reason to think he could be the one peeping through your windows, huh?"

She flashed him an exasperated glance. "Don't be ridiculous, Zack. He's been a church member here for years. We're just *friends*."

He didn't miss the emphasis on the last word. "I'm sorry," he blurted. "I'm sorry for the way I treated you last night. I was out of line."

Her jaw dropped in surprise. "Um, okay. Apology accepted."

The choir had gathered around the piano again, clearly waiting for her. "Looks like break time is over," he murmured.

"Yeah, I better get back."

"You have a beautiful voice, Merry." He flashed a smile before turning to head back to his seat.

After he sat down, he suppressed a stab of guilt. He hadn't needed to talk to Merry right then. But he'd wanted good ole Daniel to understand he was there with her.

Could he be any more obvious? He hoped Merry hadn't noticed his Neanderthal tactics.

The choir ran through a few more songs, and then suddenly Merry was singing alone, her clear voice pure and true. She sang the verse solo and the rest of the choir joined in with the refrain.

Zack was surprised when practice was over, the time going by faster than he'd anticipated. And not once had he played games on his phone.

"You didn't have to stay," Merry said as she approached. "I'm sure you were bored out of your mind."

"I wasn't bored at all," he answered honestly. "I enjoyed listening to you sing."

"Thanks," she murmured, ducking her head at the compliment, her fair skin turning pink.

He stayed beside her as they walked outside, and it took a minute for his eyes to adjust to the glare of the sun.

"Are we going back home?" Merry asked.

"I thought we'd take a little drive, first," Zack admitted. He kept his hand in the small of her back as they walked over to where he'd left his truck.

And then he saw the black Jeep.

9

"Get in," Zack urged, opening the passenger door. Merry quickly jumped in, wincing when she knocked her arm against the door frame. Zack raced around to the driver's side.

"What's wrong?" she asked as he started the truck and peeled out of the parking lot. She clicked her seatbelt into place as the truck banked around a curve.

"We need to follow that black Jeep." Zack tried to pull his seatbelt on and she reached over to help so he could keep his eyes on the road.

Merry saw the Jeep he meant, but it was already pretty far up ahead, and she found herself pressing her foot to the floor as if she had an imaginary brake. "Do you really think that's him?"

"Yes, I do. We already know Caruthers has used his friend's ID to rent the boat, so why not drive his vehicle too?"

Zack pressed steadily on the accelerator, pushing the speed limit.

A chill lifted the tiny hairs along the back of her neck.

The face in the window must have been Blake's. A small part of her didn't want to believe it. Oddly enough, she would have almost preferred some other stalker rather than knowing for sure Blake was after her again.

"Come on, where did you go?" Zack muttered, as they pulled up on the crest of a hill.

She scanned the area, looking for the Jeep even though, deep down, she didn't really want Zack to find him. "Maybe he turned off on one of the other highways?"

A muscle jumped in the corner of Zack's jaw. "I can't lose him this time."

Zack sped up and she silently prayed for their safety.

"No way! You've got to be kidding me!" Zack exclaimed in frustration.

She turned in her seat and saw the flashing red and blue lights growing brighter as the sheriff's deputy gained on them. Zack's lips thinned as he slowed down and then pulled off on the side of the highway.

"Of course I don't have my badge with me."

"Maybe once we explain about the black Jeep, you won't get a ticket." She felt bad for Zack who was only going out of his way to try and help her.

"I don't care about the speeding ticket," Zack said, reaching over to open the glove box. He pulled out the vehicle registration, and then rolled down his window. "We'll have no chance of catching up with the Jeep now."

Merry couldn't help but let out a quiet sigh of relief.

"Do you have any idea how fast you were going?" the sheriff's deputy asked.

"Yes, Officer, I was doing seventy-five in a fifty-five mile speed zone."

Merry leaned forward, trying to get a better look at the

deputy. "Deputy Armbruster? Hi, it's me, Merry Haines from the Hope County ER. How are you?"

"Merry?" Deputy Devon Armbruster bent down further so he could see her. "What are you doing with someone driving so recklessly?"

"This is Zack Crain, Julie Crain's brother," she explained. "He wasn't speeding on purpose. We were trying to catch up with a black Jeep."

Deputy Armbruster glanced between the two of them and frowned. "I guess I should have recognized you, since you resemble your sister. I'm the one who was hired after you left. Aren't you a cop in Madison, now?" he asked.

"Yes, but I took a few days off to spend time on the lake."

Merry could see the indecision reflected in the deputy's eyes. "Regardless of the reason, you were still speeding. And just because you used to be a cop here, doesn't mean I can let you off the hook."

"I know."

She had to give Zack credit for not arguing in an attempt to get out of the ticket. Of course, as a cop himself, Zack had probably heard every excuse in the book, and then some. She tried to catch Deputy Armbruster's gaze. "Listen, Deputy, you might be able to help us. You see, we have a good reason to believe that one of my former boyfriends is stalking me. We think he was driving that black Jeep. Zack was only trying to get the evidence we need to prove that Blake is violating his restraining order."

"Stalking? Restraining order?" This time Deputy Armbruster's eyebrows pulled together in a deep V. "You better come with me down to the department headquarters."

Zack scowled at her before turning back to the deputy.

"Look, I acknowledged I was speeding, you can just write me the ticket and let me go."

"Zack, we need the police to help us," she said, striving to remain calm and reasonable. "We should tell them what we know."

"Yes, you should," Deputy Armbruster agreed in a stern tone. "I'd like you to come down to headquarters, now." The deputy's tone did not offer any room for negotiation.

"Fine." Zack seemed resigned to his fate.

While Deputy Armbruster returned to his squad car, she gave Zack directions. "Make a U-turn and head back toward town."

"I know where the sheriff's department is located," he said as he proceeded to make the U-turn. "I used to work here, remember?"

"You're right, I'm sorry." She sensed he was angry with her but she didn't regret her decision to speak up. "We didn't have enough proof before, but surely we do now that we've seen the black Jeep racing away from the church parking lot."

"I bet there's more than one black Jeep in the state of Wisconsin."

"Too bad we couldn't get the license plate number," she said with a sigh.

"The Jeep was perpendicular to us in the parking lot, and by the time I got out on the road to follow him, he was too far away. You can bet I wish I had the plate number, too."

She sensed Zack was still beating himself up for not noticing the Jeep sooner. "The deputies will have a better chance of finding the Jeep than we will."

"Maybe." The doubt in Zack's tone wasn't reassuring. "Or they'll think we're crazy, seeing threats that aren't there."

She couldn't argue his point, because the first time she'd

gone to the Minneapolis police they told her she didn't have enough evidence to file a petition for a restraining order. It seemed that they didn't want to be bothered with her complaint.

It hadn't been until Blake attacked her that they'd taken her concerns seriously, although, by then, it had almost been too late.

She could only pray that the Hope County Sheriff's Department wouldn't make the same mistake. Because she knew very well just how dangerous Blake could be. Especially when he wasn't taking his psych medication.

ZACK TRIED to harness his temper as he drove to the sheriff's department. Merry was probably right to include them in what was going on, but he still couldn't help thinking that he needed more proof before going to the sheriff's department.

Merry kept glancing at him, clearly worried, so he forced himself to let go of his frustration. "I'm sorry. I'm not upset with you. I just wish I could have at least gotten close enough to get his tag number."

"I understand." Merry's smile was a bit strained, and he mentally kicked himself for being a jerk. "But, you have to understand that I'm worried about you, too. By now, Blake knows that you're spending time with me, and he's not going to like that. You think he'll come after me, but if that were true, he's already had plenty of time to make his move. Now that he has seen you hanging around, I'm worried he's more likely to take his anger out on you."

Zack was deeply touched by her concern for his welfare. He hadn't wanted to get involved, but he knew that he'd do whatever was necessary to keep Merry safe. "Hey, I'm happy to hear that he might come after me. As far as I'm concerned, that's way better than going after you."

Merry rolled her eyes, but didn't say anything more as he pulled into the parking lot of the sheriff's department. Deputy Armbruster was standing near the door waiting for them with a serious expression on his face.

Zack climbed out from behind the wheel and joined Merry to walk up to the building.

"Follow me," Deputy Armbruster said.

Blessedly cool air washed over him as they walked inside. Deputy Armbruster led them over to a small conference area, gesturing for them to take a seat.

"Now then," Deputy Armbruster said as he pulled out a small notebook. "Why don't you start at the very beginning?"

Zack nodded for Merry to start. She did her best to give the short version, describing how she'd dated Caruthers, but when he turned violent took out a restraining order against him.

"And what makes you think this Blake guy is in Crystal Lake?" Armbruster asked.

Now it was Zack's turn to describe how he'd found the boot print beneath the bedroom window. He pulled out his phone and showed Armbruster the photo he'd taken, and then described the redhead they saw on the lake. "We're fairly certain Blake has rented a fishing boat under the name of Calvin Reynolds, who apparently spent time with Caruthers in prison. We also believe the black Jeep we were following belongs to Reynolds as well, although we didn't get the plate number yet."

He'd caught Armbruster's attention now. "So you believe Caruthers is here, pretending to be Reynolds in order to harm Merry?"

The familiar use of Merry's first name wasn't lost on Zack. She must know him pretty well from his frequent visits to the ER. "Yes, I do. I've been doing my best to protect her, which is why I drove her to choir practice."

"I see." Deputy Armbruster turned toward Merry. "Have you been able to identify Caruthers?"

Merry slowly shook her head. "Not exactly. He has bright red hair, but he's always been too far away to get a clear look at his face. Even yesterday, when I saw his face pressed up against the kitchen window, he had his hands cupped around it, and the image was so fleeting I couldn't swear under oath that it was really him."

Deputy Armbruster slapped his notebook shut. "That's enough to convince me," he declared. "I'll see what I can dig up on this guy Reynolds. We'll be able to get his tag number from the system and from there we'll put out an all points bulletin for the rest of the deputies to keep an eye out for him."

Zack couldn't hide his surprise. "Thank you. I have to tell you that one of the Madison cops, Colton Wallace, has been helping me investigate, too. He's trying to find Calvin Reynolds to validate that he loaned his driver's license, credit card and Jeep to Caruthers."

"Good, I'd like you to keep me updated on what Wallace uncovers." Armbruster pulled out his business card and handed it over. "Call me any time."

Bemused, Zack tucked the card in his wallet. "I will."

He'd told Merry that he thought the sheriff's department would likely take her concerns more seriously, but he hadn't expected it to be this easy. Clearly Deputy Armbruster cared about Merry, although he didn't get the vibe that the deputy wanted to date her. More that he cared about her like a sister.

Zack tried to remember the last time he'd felt remotely involved with any of his victims in Madison. He always took his job of bringing criminals to justice seriously, but he'd kept his emotions deeply hidden. A much easier task in a big city like Madison compared to the small town of Crystal Lake.

"Thank you, Deputy," Merry said, taking his hand in hers. "I'm glad to know that you'll be looking out for Blake."

The tips of Deputy Armbruster's ears turned bright red, and Zack revised his previous opinion. Armbruster didn't consider Merry a sister at all. He was just too polite to flirt with her while on duty. Or in front of Zack.

Zack's gut clenched at the thought of Merry finding someone else to share her life with. There were plenty of single men in Crystal Lake, and even in Madison, who'd obviously like to date her. Colton, Daniel, and even Deputy Armbruster. Men who wouldn't balk at the idea of giving her what she deserved, including marriage and a family.

He never should have kissed her. No matter how much he'd wanted to. No matter how much he'd enjoyed holding her. No matter how much he thought about kissing her again.

Now that the sheriff's department was on the case, Zack figured it wouldn't take long for them to find the black Jeep and, hopefully, arrest Caruthers, sending him back to jail or to a psychiatric hospital where he really belonged.

And the minute that happened, he wouldn't need to stay in Crystal Lake any longer. He could return home, avoiding the sweet temptation of kissing Merry.

But for some odd reason, the idea of leaving Merry

alone, even once Caruthers was no longer a threat, didn't make him feel better.

In fact, the ache of loneliness in his chest only seemed to spread, encapsulating his heart.

MERRY WAS RELIEVED to know that Deputy Armbruster whole-heartedly believed them, and he'd never given Zack the speeding ticket. In fact, Deputy Armbruster seemed to be a man on a mission to find Blake and to bring him to justice.

Once they were back in Zack's truck, her stomach rumbled loud enough for him to hear, judging by the quick glance he sent her way.

"How about we eat lunch at Rose's Café?" he suggested. "It's well past noon, and I know you're probably as hungry as I am."

She was surprised by his offer and refusing seemed pointless, considering her grumbling stomach. "That would be great, thanks."

Neither one of them said much on the trip into town but Zack's previous sense of urgency to find Caruthers seemed to have evaporated. She wondered if he was secretly relieved to have handed the investigation off to the sheriff's department. After all, Zack had taken a few days off work to relax and enjoy the lake, not to work.

Merry found it hard to believe that just a few days had passed since Leonard had knocked her against the nurse's station. Being in Zack's company these past few days had changed her. She glanced at his handsome profile, remembering their heated kiss. She told herself that she had purposefully avoided relationships over these past two years, but now realized that wasn't true.

At Julie and Derek's wedding, she'd been immediately attracted to Zack, even though she knew he was still grieving the loss of his wife and daughter. But now that he'd kissed her, she understood that she wasn't interested in other men because she cared about Zack.

Far more than she should.

There was nothing she could do though, if Zack didn't return her feelings. Was this how Blake had felt when she explained she didn't love him? She couldn't help the flash of guilt. She tried to concentrate on scoping out a parking space, which were nonexistent on a Saturday afternoon with all the summer tourists flocking to the lake.

"We'll have to walk a ways," Zack said as he reached the end of Main Street. "I should have just stayed in the sheriff's department parking lot. We could have walked from there just as easily."

"I don't mind walking. I've been feeling like a slug, and I obviously won't be able to do my usual exercise routine for the next few weeks."

"All right." Zack parked the truck and pocketed his keys. They walked back up Main Street, weaving around tourists to make their way to Rose's Café.

Merry hoped it was just her imagination that made her feel like everyone inside the Café stared at them as they walked in. Having lunch with Zack two days in a row would surely start the small town tongues wagging. Then she spotted Dr. Katy's auburn hair across the room and rushed over.

"Hi, Dr. Katy."

"Merry!" Dr. Katy gave her a quick hug. "I'm so glad to see that you're feeling better."

"I'm fine. But tell me, how is Leonard? I know you managed to sedate him, but I'm hoping he didn't have to end up being transferred to the psych hospital in Madison."

Dr. Katy's smile faded. "Unfortunately, that is where he ended up. When we finally tracked down his mother Doreen, she was in the cafeteria and had no idea how she'd gotten there. I conferred with several of my colleagues and we agreed she wasn't capable of taking care of Leonard any longer."

"Oh no, that's terrible," Merry whispered. She'd been praying for Leonard and his mother, but hearing that he might have to spend the rest of his life in a psych hospital was discouraging. "I feel so awful for what happened."

"It's not your fault." Dr. Katy's smile was sad. "Most physicians across the country will agree that the current way of providing psychiatric care isn't meeting the needs of our patients. I know locking up Leonard isn't the answer, but most halfway house facilities don't want to take a chance on taking him in because of his history of violent outbursts. It's a lose-lose situation all the way around."

Merry knew Dr. Katy was right, but that didn't make her feel any better. "I know, thanks for the update."

She turned around to join Zack, only to find him right behind her. The dejected expression on his face confirmed that he'd overheard Dr. Katy's remarks.

"I'm sorry to hear about Leonard," he murmured as they slid into a vacant booth.

"It's not your fault any more than it's mine," Merry pointed out. "All we can do now is pray for him."

"Okay." Zack shocked her by bowing his head. "Dear

Lord, we ask You to heal Leonard and to provide him the comfort he deserves, Amen."

She stared at Zack in shock, awed and humbled that he'd pray for Leonard when he hadn't prayed for himself.

And in that moment, she began to hope that Zack might just find his way back to faith and God after all.

10

Zack wasn't sure why he'd felt the need to pray for Leonard, other than he felt guilty for the role he'd played in the poor guy ending up locked up in a psychiatric hospital. But the pleased expression on Merry's face made him feel good. As if she approved.

However, mere seconds later, the familiar guilt began to creep in. He knew he was fast losing control of the situation, but somehow he couldn't seem to make himself stop the downward spiral. Praying had opened up a fissure in his heart he'd thought he'd firmly cemented shut. But, thankfully, he didn't feel the same deep, stabbing pain that he had during those first few months after losing Amelia and Suz.

A sign that he was finally healing, the way their church pastor had once told him he would? Maybe. But Zack wasn't certain that it was a positive sign.

Shouldn't a man who'd promised to love and honor his wife stay true to her, even after she was gone? Was he betraying Suz by wanting to kiss Merry? And what about his daughter? How could he ever bring more children into the world after losing Amelia? No child could ever replace Amelia in his heart.

He scrubbed his hands over his face, trying not to panic. Feeling was one thing, but considering getting involved again in a relationship, was something else.

He so wasn't ready for that.

"Thank you, Zack," Merry said softly, breaking into his internal monologue. "I appreciate you praying for Leonard."

He forced a smile and tried not to take his emotional turmoil out on her. "Yeah, well, he needs all the support he can get."

"So do you."

Her words were soft, but they scrapped across his skin like a wire brush. It was all he could do not to snap at her, like a wounded animal caught in a trap.

He took a deep breath, fighting for control. "Are you ready to order?" He dropped his gaze to the plastic menu he'd once known by heart. "I'm thinking of having meatloaf."

There was a long pause, and he refused to look up at her, unwilling to see the hurt reflected in her amber eyes. He was deeply relieved when their young server, Darcy, chose that moment to sashay over holding two water glasses.

"Hi, Zack. What a nice surprise to see you two days in a row."

"Hey, Darcy, how have you been?" The moment the question spewed out, he wished he could take it back, especially when her entire face brightened.

"I'm doing really well! I'm heading back to UW Madison to complete my senior year next week." She tipped her head in a move that was probably supposed to be coy. "Maybe we can catch up some time?"

"I always work a lot of hours, but we'll see." He just

couldn't quite tell her no outright, even though he wasn't the least bit tempted to see Darcy on a personal level. "Tell us what the specials are for today."

Darcy didn't seem at all deterred by his refusal to commit to a future date. She rattled through the specials, hardly sparing Merry a glance. Darcy's rudeness was so obvious, he couldn't stand it.

"Merry, what sounds good to you?" he asked, purposefully including her in the conversation.

"Um, I don't know." Merry seemed overly preoccupied with her menu, too, and he knew he had only himself to blame. "I guess I'll have the egg salad sandwich."

"Great. I'll have the meatloaf. Thanks, Darcy." Zack handed over the menus, hoping Darcy would get the hint and move on.

"Okay, let me know if you need anything." The way Darcy put an obvious swing in her walk as she went back to the kitchen to put in their order made him wince.

"What's Darcy's major?" Merry asked, breaking the strained silence.

"No clue." And frankly, he didn't care. "She's younger than Julie, you know."

Merry lifted an eyebrow as if to say so what? He shook his head and tried to think of a way to change the subject. Again.

"When is your next doctor's appointment?" Surely Merry's health was a safe subject.

"Next week Thursday, but I'm not hopeful that anything will change. I have a feeling I'll be off work for a while yet."

It bothered him to realize he wouldn't be here to find out for himself what the outcome of her follow-up appointment would be. "Check with your boss. Since you were injured at work, there's a good chance that they'll bring you back even if it means doing some sort of light-duty work."

"Really?" Merry's gaze widened with hope. "That would be awesome. I can't bear the thought of sitting in my apartment for six to eight weeks. I'll take light-duty work over that any time."

A reluctant smile tugged at the corner of his mouth. Trust Merry to be one of the few who didn't want to be forced off work.

Which unfortunately, only made him admire her more.

MERRY TRIED to ignore Darcy's obvious flirting, but it wasn't easy. The only saving grace was that Zack hadn't seemed interested in her, although the way he'd totally shut down after praying for Leonard was upsetting. She had the distinct feeling that if he could take his hastily spoken prayer back, he would.

She was grateful when the meal was finally over. But before they could leave the diner, Zack was stopped by a couple of guys she didn't know.

"Zack! Great to see you're back in town, man!" A tall guy slapped Zack on the shoulder, and she wondered if they'd gone to school together.

"Are you here all weekend?" the shorter guy asked.

"Yep, here until Monday."

"Perfect," the first guy exclaimed. "We're playing softball at two o'clock this afternoon and we could use another player. Why don't you join us? It'll be just like old times."

Merry shouldn't have been surprised to hear that Zack

had once played softball. When he hesitated and glanced back at her she stepped forward. "That's a great idea."

Zack still looked uncertain. "Are you sure you won't mind sitting and watching?"

"Of course not. We could run back to the townhouse first and pick up Ace, if you think there's time."

The smile that bloomed on Zack's face warmed her heart. "All right, that would be awesome."

"So you're gonna play?" the first guy asked.

"Yep, I'll be there." Zack took a step back in order to bring her into the group. "Merry, I'd like you to meet Tony Delarosa and Kade Thompson, two guys I played ball with in high school. Tony and Kade, this is Merry Haines. She's one of the ER nurses at Hope County Hospital."

"Nice to meet you," she murmured as the two men stared at her with blatant curiosity.

"Likewise," Tony said with a wide grin. "You've been holding out on us, Crain."

"Oh no, we're just friends," Merry quickly interjected.

The way Tony and Kade exchanged amused glances made her realize they were just teasing. She blushed and realized she was way out of practice when it came to dealing with men.

"See you guys later," Zack said, putting his hand behind her back and nudging her toward the door.

She didn't need to be asked twice. Outside, the sidewalk along Main Street was even more crowded than when they arrived. Zack held her right hand and pushed his way through the mass of people, and she did her best to follow along behind him, even though she was jostled with almost every step.

Finally, the crowds thinned and they were able to walk side by side to the spot where Zack had left his truck. He didn't let go of her hand, though, until he'd opened the passenger door for her.

"Thanks." Getting into the high truck was awkward without the full use of her left arm, but she managed to ignore the pain to avoid being lifted by Zack. Her emotions were already out of whack from spending so much time with him.

"Are you sure you don't mind sitting outside to watch the game?" he asked, throwing the truck into gear and backing out of the parking space. "Because I don't have to play if you're tired and need to rest."

"I'd like to watch you guys play," she said, striving to keep her tone light. "Should be fun."

He didn't look as if he believed her, and she wondered if he was having second thoughts about agreeing to participate. Well too bad. She wasn't about to give him an excuse to back out. Zack needed this impromptu afternoon ball game more than she did.

When they arrived at the townhouse, Zack made her wait in the locked truck with the air conditioning running while he walked around to make sure Blake wasn't lurking nearby. Zack let Ace outside, and then came back for her.

"We should pack a little cooler of soft drinks, and maybe some snacks," Zack suggested. "I have a portable canvas chair for you, and we'll need to bring Ace's water dish, too. There are some shady areas, but I'm afraid he'll get too hot sitting outside in the sun."

For a guy who seemed inclined to duck out of the game, he was doing a lot in the way of preparations.

"Okay, anything else?"

Zack paused, but then shook his head. "That should do it. Stay here and I'll get everything together."

She sat in the shade on the front porch with Ace as Zack

packed his truck. When she saw the size of the cooler, she wondered if they were providing soft drinks and water for every guy on the team.

Zack glanced at her, and then snapped his fingers. "I almost forgot sunscreen." Without waiting for a response he headed back inside, returning again a few minutes later.

Merry rose to her feet. "I don't know why you need sunscreen. You're already tan from being out in the sun."

"It's not for me, Freckles, it's for you. Are you ready?"

She rolled her eyes at the unoriginal nickname. "Yes, I'm ready. Come on, Ace."

The shadows that had darkened his eyes before lunch vanished as Zack drove to the Crystal Lake Park. She'd hoped that praying would help him find his way back to God, but for some reason, it had seemed to have the opposite effect.

At times, Zack's emotions seemed to be all over the place, and for a moment she was reminded of Blake. Not that she believed that Zack had any type of psychiatric disorder, but he still went hot and cold in a matter of seconds.

She didn't understand him, or maybe she just didn't get men in general. Several of her nursing friends had complained about their significant others not being faithful, or that they were self-absorbed or just plain not very nice.

All she knew about Zack was what she heard from Julie, who was obviously biased when it came to the older brother she idolized. She had no idea what sort of a husband or father he had been.

Clearly, he'd loved his wife and daughter, but it was also possible that he was grieving even more out of a sense of guilt. Maybe he hadn't always been there for them. Maybe he had other regrets.

Blake had damaged her physically and emotionally. It had taken years to gain her self-confidence back. Did she really want to risk being hurt again by Zack Crain? A man who'd told her more than once that he didn't have anything to offer her.

No, she didn't.

Better to focus on being his friend, helping him to find his way back to God and faith, but nothing more.

ZACK GAVE Tony's bat several practice swings, glad to be doing something physically challenging. He didn't have any of his gear here, so the guys had supplied him with their spare stuff.

The glove he was given wasn't nearly as good as his, but it would do. The guys had divided up into two teams and had done rock, paper, scissors to see who would be first at bat.

His and Tony's team had won.

He handed the bat over to Tony, and then glanced back to look for Merry. She'd found a shady spot beneath a tree to sit and watch the game. With the cooler at her side, a cold bottle of water in her hand and Ace curled up at her feet, she looked perfectly happy.

The guys had razzed him about Merry, but he'd repeated her story since she'd seemed anxious to make sure they knew the truth. For his sake? Or hers? There was no reason on earth that she couldn't date one of them. Except for the fact that he wouldn't like it.

Really, this ridiculous fascination with Merry's potential

love life had to stop. She deserved better than him. His head knew that, but his heart was being stubborn.

Tony hit a double and stood on second base, grinning like an idiot. Zack shook his head wryly and stepped up to the plate to bat next. He did his best to focus on the pitch rather than thinking about Merry.

The first pitch was outside, but their makeshift umpire called it a strike. Zack scowled, tugged his baseball cap down further over his eyes, and decided he couldn't afford to be too picky.

The next pitch wasn't perfect either, but he swung as hard as he could. The bat hit the ball with a resounding crack, sending it sailing over the heads of the outfielders who were scrambling to back up. A home run! Tony made it home first and when Zack rounded second base, he saw that Merry was on her feet cheering for him while Ace barked loudly, clearly not sure what was going on but unwilling to be left out.

He was pleasantly surprised and touched that she cared enough to root for him and couldn't help but grin, no doubt looking just as goofy as Tony had on his double. Zack lifted his hand in a wave as he hit third base, and then sailed over home plate.

Their brief moment of fame was quickly derailed when the other team went up to bat and hit several home runs as well. Zack played second base and made several good plays. Apparently his high school baseball skills hadn't totally abandoned him.

The game was loud and fun, both sides scoring many points before they finally called it quits after five innings and nearly a tie score. Everyone hung around guzzling sports drinks and munchies. Merry joined the group, leaving Ace in the shade of the tree.

"Nice game," she said. "I had fun watching."

Zack swiped his sweaty face with a towel, trying to keep downwind from Merry to spare her the stench. "It was a blast, although it's too bad we're not closer to the lake so I could take a quick swim before heading home. I'm afraid I don't smell the greatest."

"I'm a nurse. Trust me, I've smelled far worse."

He chuckled and glanced over at Ace. "We better get going. I think Ace is feeling left out."

"All right."

He glanced back at Tony and Kade. "Hey guys, we're taking off."

"Try not to be a stranger," Kade said, giving him a playful smack in the shoulder. "We have these ball games often during the summer and you're always welcome."

Zack couldn't remember the last time he'd hung out with any of his old friends. Certainly, they'd hung out in the early days, when he and Suz were dating. But after they'd gotten married and had Amelia, he hadn't bothered to keep in touch.

That was on him, and to be honest he wasn't sure if he had to go back in time that he wouldn't do the same thing again. He'd liked being married. He liked having a family.

But there was something to be said for having friends, too.

He followed Merry over to where Ace was standing and whining beneath the tree. When she bent down to untie the dog's leash, he noticed a slip of paper hanging out of the side pocket of her jeans.

"Look out, you're going to lose this," he said, gesturing to the slip of paper.

"I don't even know what it is." Merry frowned as she

pulled the paper out and, suddenly, the color leeched from her face.

"What's wrong?" He took the slip of paper from her fingers and had to control the flash of fury when he saw it was a note from Caruthers.

We'll be together again, soon, Meredith.

Love, Blake.

11

Merry struggled to maintain her composure as she swiped her hands on the seat of her jeans. Just touching the note Blake had stuffed in her pocket made her feel like taking another shower.

"When did he get this into your pocket?" Zack demanded.

She shook her head and shrugged her right shoulder. "No one has been anywhere near me since we arrived in the park. But when we walked through town, we were surrounded by people. I have to assume that's when he slipped the note to me.

Zack scowled and glanced around the park, clearly searching for some sign of Blake. "I don't like this," he said in a grim tone. "I think we'd better head back to the sheriff's department and see if they have any leads. It shouldn't be this difficult to find him."

Silently agreeing with him, she swallowed hard against a wave of despair. She didn't understand why Blake had remained obsessed with her, especially after all this time had passed. She closed her eyes and prayed.

Please, Lord, keep us safe in Your care. And please help heal Blake, too. Amen.

She opened her eyes, relieved at the sense of calmness that wafted over her. She turned toward Zack, who was staring at her intently. She smiled. "I'm ready to leave if you are."

"I'm amazed how well praying seems to work for you," Zack said in a low voice. "One minute I thought you were ready to fall apart, and then next you appear calm and serene."

"Praying does give me peace," she admitted. "Facing fear is easier when I remember I'm not alone."

Zack seemed intrigued by the idea, but then Ace began to bark again and he quickly looked around, as if sensing a threat. But this time Ace was only barking at another dog, a small Westie being walked by a young girl along the edge of the park.

"Not your type, Ace," Zack said wryly. He turned to Merry. "Take the dog's leash and I'll grab the cooler."

Merry took the leash and shortened it up, since Ace seemed determined to get to know the Westie better. "Stay, Ace. Stay."

As usual, the dog didn't listen to her very well. They made their way to Zack's truck, and from there drove straight to the sheriff's department.

They arrived after the shift change, so Deputy Armbruster wasn't available, but Deputy Thomas agreed to talk to them.

"Hi, Merry." Deputy Thomas had stopped by the hospital many times, so she knew him almost as well as she knew Deputy Armbruster. "I heard about your stalker, but don't worry, we're going to catch him."

"With all the guys you have looking for him, I would

have hoped you'd picked him up already," Zack said grimly. "He's already gotten too close to Merry."

Deputy Thomas frowned. "What do you mean?"

"Read this." Zack held out the note Blake had managed to stuff into her pocket.

"When did you get this?" Deputy Thomas asked in a grim tone.

"I don't know for sure," Merry admitted. "We walked up and down Main Street this afternoon and the sidewalk was jam packed with people. He must have slipped it into my pocket, most likely after we left Rose's Café."

"Look, Deputy, I don't like the way he's watching her," Zack said, his gaze troubled. "You need to find him before he escalates."

"I understand your concern, and trust me, we are looking for him. But we also have other calls we're taking as well. We've already busted up a big fight at Barry's Pub, not to mention being called out to a couple of car crashes. Weekends are busy around here, especially in the height of tourist season."

"I know you're busy," Merry spoke up, trying to smooth over Zack's rough tone. "And I really appreciate everything you're doing for me."

"We'll do our best to find him," Deputy Thomas assured her. "We take care of our own."

She was pleased he'd included her as belonging to Crystal Lake even though she hadn't grown up here the way Julie and Zack had. The moment she'd arrived, she'd fallen in love with the small town and the beautiful lake. There were acres of woods just a few miles away, and she'd seen dozens of deer in the past few years.

"Thank you," she said.

"Have you been through the campsite?" Zack asked.

"I know Deputy Armbruster drove through," Deputy Thomas admitted. "But I think that was about the time he was called away to break up the fight. I'll head over there soon, and we all have the tag number of the black Jeep."

"I appreciate that," Zack said.

"Merry, I'd like to keep the note as evidence," Deputy Thomas said. "We're not likely to get prints, but we could always have a handwriting analysis done if needed."

Since she didn't want to see the note again, she wasn't about to argue. "No problem."

"Thanks again," Zack said as they turned to leave.

Zack seemed to be deep in thought as they walked back to the truck. She found herself wishing that he'd give prayer another try, because she was convinced he'd feel so much better if he shared his burden with God.

But she couldn't force him, either. Faith was something he had to accept on his own. And she had a feeling that Zack wouldn't be able to find his faith until he finally let go of his sorrow over losing his wife and daughter.

She wanted Zack to have peace, even if he couldn't bear to open himself up to love again.

Zack kept a sharp lookout for any sign of Caruthers as he drove back to his sister's townhouse. He still couldn't believe that the guy had gotten close enough to Merry to slip a note in her pocket.

Thankfully, Caruthers hadn't done anything worse.

Dear Lord, please keep Merry safe!

The prayer popped into his mind almost automatically, the way he used to talk to God before he'd lost his family.

Two prayers in one day. And he didn't regret them, either. For whatever reason he found it easier to pray for others, like Leonard and especially for Merry, than it was to pray for himself.

Would God listen to his prayers? Maybe, especially since both Leonard and Merry were truly deserving of God's love and protection.

Zack was tempted to drive through the campsite himself, but at the same time, didn't want to expose Merry to any further danger. Better for Thomas to do that, so he could go ahead and arrest Caruthers if he saw him or the Jeep. At least the note provided the proof they needed that Caruthers had violated his restraining order.

He pulled in front of his sister's townhouse and decided to walk Merry and Ace up to the house before grabbing the cooler. Maybe he was being a bit on the paranoid side, but better safe than sorry.

A quick search confirmed that the house was empty. As he was dragging the cooler inside, his cell phone rang. He set the cooler down in front of the kitchen sink and reached for the phone.

"Hey Cole, what's up?"

"Just giving you a status report," his buddy said. "Unfortunately, we still haven't found Calvin Reynolds. And he didn't show up for his bartender shift at the local tavern, either."

Zack couldn't ignore the sudden chill that snaked down his spine. "Do you think it's possible Caruthers murdered him?"

"Too early to tell. For all we know the two men are

together," Cole pointed out. "But yeah, it's definitely suspicious."

Zack wholeheartedly agreed. "I don't suppose a missing persons report was filed?"

"Not yet, but if we don't find any sign of him by tomorrow, then we may do that. I'll send over a driver's license photo of the guy, just in case he is there with Caruthers."

"Thanks, I'll be sure to share it with the deputies here."

"You have the locals involved?" Cole asked.

"Yeah. I didn't have much of a choice since I was stopped for speeding while we were trying to follow the black Jeep."

Cole chuckled. "Would love to have been there to see that."

"Do you have any other information?" Zack asked.

"Nope. As soon as we hang up you'll get the photo."

"Thanks, Cole," Zack said in a serious tone. "For covering my shifts and for the help."

"You know how you can pay me back," Cole teased. "Introduce me to pretty Merry and we'll call it even."

"Fat chance," Zack said half under his breath. "Bye." He disconnected the call, the sound of his buddy's laughter still ringing in his ears.

True to Colton's word, a text message came through a few seconds later. He stared at the grainy photograph of Calvin Reynolds, trying to remember if he'd seen the guy even in passing. Judging by the size of his thick neck, Reynolds was heavier than Caruthers, and with his long stringy brown hair and black eyebrow piercing, the guy would easily stand out in a crowd.

Zack still had Armbruster's contact information so he forwarded the photo to him asking him to share it with the rest of the deputies. Satisfied that they had another clue to go on, he began cleaning out the cooler.

"I can help," Merry said, coming up to stand beside him. Her sweet vanilla scent reminded him that he probably reeked like sweat and needed to take a shower.

"I'll finish this," he said. "You might want to stand back until I can get cleaned up."

"Don't be silly," she said exasperation echoing through her tone. "How about we work together? Set the soft drinks and snacks on the counter and I'll put them away while you drain the water out of the bottom of the cooler."

For some reason her bossy tone made him smile. "Is this why you're the ER charge nurse? Because you like to give orders?"

"Absolutely." She opened the fridge and held it open with her hip as she tucked the leftovers inside.

The desire to kiss her again was nearly overwhelming, and he was glad when the cooler was finally empty and he had a good excuse to go outside.

He liked Merry, far too much for his own good. Working together with her in the kitchen only emphasized the loneliness surrounding him.

His choice, he reminded himself. Yet at the same time, he couldn't help thinking that it could also be his choice to change his approach.

He could decide to share his life with others rather than keeping himself isolated from his friends and his family. He could even go as far as to widen his circle of friends.

After dumping the cooler upside down on the grass, he glanced toward the lake to where his boat was tied up beneath the canopy of the boat lift. An evening boat ride would be the perfect end to a great day. He and Merry could pack up the leftovers from the afternoon and last night's grilling and stay out on the water long enough to watch the sunset.

Was he out of his mind to take Merry out on what any normal person would consider a date?

Maybe. But there was no denying that he enjoyed spending time with her. That he wanted to see her laugh, to watch the expression of awe on her face as they watched the sun dip behind the horizon.

And for the first time in a long time, he let go of the pain and sorrow.

MERRY WATCHED through the patio doors as Zack dried out the cooler. His mood had once again shifted so that he seemed lighter and happier.

She wondered how he would feel about going to church with her in the morning. Obviously, she had to go since she was singing in the choir. But would he stay again, like he did today? Or would sitting through an entire service be too much for him?

"I'll be right next door if you need me," Zack called through the screen door. "Keep Ace with you, okay?"

"Okay." Ace had settled down in front of the door, as if a bit worn out by spending the afternoon at the park.

Suddenly exhausted, Merry curled up in the corner of the sofa, rested her head against the cushion and closed her eyes. She wished she could spend more time with Zack. Sooner or later he'd open up and let God's love shine through, and she found that she wanted to be there when that happened.

Was that being selfish? She didn't like to think so. It was

just that while watching Zack play softball she caught a glimpse of the man he used to be.

The man he could be again.

It struck her that his moodiness was more likely related to his struggles with faith, rather than having anything to do with her, personally. She hoped that Pastor John's service would somehow find its way through Zack's internal barriers.

She must have dozed again because she woke up when she heard Zack calling her name. "Merry? Are you all right?"

"I'm fine," she said, putting her hand up to smooth her tangled hair. "Took a little cat nap, that's all."

He frowned in concern. "Are you still having headaches?"

"No headaches, just this weird exhaustion that hits me out of nowhere." She stood, and then crossed over to the patio door where Ace stood wagging his tail in a way that convinced her he wanted to go outside. She opened the door and smiled as Ace bounded out to do his doggy business. Zack's dark hair was damp, and he wore a clean pair of canvas shorts and a green T-shirt that mirrored the color of his eyes. The scent of his aftershave reminded her of their all-too-brief kiss.

He was so handsome, her heart ached with longing.

"Do you think you're up for an evening boat ride?" Zack asked hesitantly. "If not, it's no big deal. I just thought it would be nice to watch the sunset over the lake."

"That sounds wonderful!" She didn't even try to hide her enthusiasm. "I'd love to go for an evening boat ride."

"Great." Zack's boyish grin went straight to her heart. "I thought we'd pack up our leftovers from last night in case we get hungry later."

She opened the door to let Ace back in. "Sounds perfect. When do you want to leave?"

"Any time you're ready."

"Just give me a few minutes to freshen up." She was feeling more than a little self-conscious about her wrinkled clothes and tangled hair, especially considering how Zack had cleaned up.

"No rush. I'll use the time to pull the leftovers together."

She nodded and slipped down the hall towards the bathroom located right outside the guest bedroom. Even though she knew better, she couldn't help thinking of this little outing as their first date.

And more than anything, she didn't want it to be the last.

THIRTY-FIVE MINUTES LATER, Merry settled into the seat beside Zack as they headed out over the lake in his speedboat. Zack had insisted on bringing Ace along, since the dog clearly didn't want to be left behind. Ace settled in the back of the boat like a sailing pro.

Merry noticed that Zack set a slow but steady pace, even though she'd be willing to bet he normally preferred speed. "You don't have to go slow just for me," she pointed out.

He flashed a wide grin. "Yes, I do, you're still recovering from your concussion. Besides, I don't mind. As soon as the sun goes down, it will be a no wake zone for the entire lake anyway."

She didn't understand all the boating rules, but since Zack seemed happy enough she let the subject drop. His kind consideration warmed her more than she cared to admit. He made a circle around the lake, glancing frequently at the *For Sale* signs.

"Are you thinking of buying?" she asked, when he slowed almost to a complete stop in front of one place.

He looked at her and nodded slowly. "Yeah, I've been thinking about it. Although it seems ridiculous since I can only get up here on the occasional weekend off work."

Merry tried to ignore the leap of her heart at the thought of Zack spending more time in Crystal Lake. "It's not silly at all, having both quiet time and fun time is important."

"Yeah, maybe. Although I'm not sure if I can even afford any lake property at this point. I'm sure the prices have skyrocketed over the past few years."

"Julie and Derek are thinking of selling the townhouse next year," she offered. "Maybe an investment property would help pay some of the bills?"

He looked shocked at the news. "I didn't know they were thinking of selling."

She bit her lower lip, hoping she hadn't let out any secrets. "Julie mentioned that they want to be in their own house before they have more children. Or maybe she was just thinking out loud."

"Something to consider," Zack said softly. "Although renting out the other side of the townhouse is no guarantee."

"They had a renter for a while, but then the doctor quit the hospital to move back to Madison. Apparently, the life-style here was just too quiet for him."

"Some people love it and others don't."

"I'm in the love it category," she said, enjoying the cool breeze washing over them as Zack sped up a bit. "I hope they catch Blake soon, because I don't want to have to move again."

"We'll get him," Zack said with confidence. "Don't even think of moving. Running isn't the answer."

It was on the tip of her tongue to mention that Zack had run away to Madison to avoid the constant reminder of his wife and daughter, but just then the edge of the sun touched the horizon and the bright yellow light shifted to a deep orange.

"Look, Zack, isn't it beautiful?"

Zack shut down the boat motor so that they drifted along on the waves, the gentle rocking motion more relaxing than anything she'd ever experienced before. No wonder some people slept on their boats.

For several long minutes, they simply gazed at the glorious sunset. When the boat drifted sideways, Merry stood and turned so she could better see the colorful sky.

She was so focused on the sunset that she didn't notice the larger wave from a passing boat coming toward them until it hit the boat, making the vessel rock sharply beneath her feet. She would have fallen if Zack hadn't stood up and caught her in his arms.

"Thank you," she murmured breathlessly. Being held in his arms caused her heart to race so fast it was a wonder she didn't have a full-out cardiac arrest.

"Merry," Zack whispered mere moments before he lowered his head and kissed her.

12

Merry clung to Zack's shoulder with her right arm, reveling in his kiss. He mouth was gentle yet firm, and the way he kissed her so tenderly while holding her close made her want to cry.

Zack was so different from Blake. Even though they'd only spent a few days together, she already instinctively knew Zack would never hurt her physically. In fact, she trusted Zack with her life.

But emotionally, not so much. Not that Zack would intentionally try to hurt her, but his wounds hadn't healed and the scars from losing his wife and daughter might be too deep for her to overcome.

As much as she cared about Zack, she couldn't deny that he hadn't made any promises. There was a good chance he wouldn't allow himself to have any sort of future. Not to mention, he hadn't fully embraced his faith. Merry knew she couldn't replace his wife and his daughter in his heart. Truthfully, she didn't want to. But she didn't think Zack would allow himself to care for her, either. Or for anyone else.

This time, she was the one who broke off the kiss, easing backward until he lifted his head and dropped his arms. He stared down at her in confusion, and even though she couldn't see his eyes in the dim light she sensed she'd hurt him.

"Zack, I...care about you," she said in a low voice. "But last night you told me you can't give me what I need. And I don't think anything has changed since then, has it?"

Zack let out a heavy sigh, lifted his hand to rub the back of his neck while he looked away. "Probably not," he agreed.

She tried to smile as if her heart wasn't breaking. "I didn't think so."

"Actually, that's not exactly true," Zack corrected, abruptly swinging back around to face her. "You need to understand that for the first time in years, I feel happy. The time we've spent together has been wonderful and fun. I don't understand why, but I feel as if the heavy weight on my shoulders has lightened a bit."

A fissure of hope opened in her heart. "I thought you seemed happier since the last time I saw you, but I wasn't sure if that was just wishful thinking on my part."

"It's not your imagination, it's true." He looked pensive for a minute and even though they were missing the glorious sunset, she didn't glance away from him. "I guess it's no secret that I bottled up all my feelings, keeping them locked away as if I didn't have the right to be happy after losing Suzanne and Amelia."

She nodded, encouraging him to continue.

"I guess I just haven't been able to understand why I'm here while they're gone."

"Oh Zack, I know you've suffered more than anyone should have to, but you need to remember that God has a plan for you." Merry prayed that she'd find the right words to help him understand. "It's not really up to us to question God's will, is it? All we can do is to ask for the Lord's strength and wisdom to guide us through the difficult times."

"I don't know, maybe," he hedged.

She knew she was right, but it was clear he wasn't yet in full agreement. There had to be another way. "Suzanne loved you, didn't she?"

He looked surprised. "Yes, of course."

"And I know how much you loved her. Tell me, what if the situation was reversed? What if you'd passed away and Suzanne was alone? Wouldn't you have wanted her to find love and happiness again?"

"Of course I would," he agreed readily. "But that's a completely different situation. Suzanne would deserve to have someone love her and to take care of her."

"And you don't?" She didn't understand his reasoning.

"I'm not sure I'd survive another loss," he said in a low tone. "And somehow, the thought of having a family makes me feel like I've turned my back on the one I had."

She suppressed a sigh. "I'm sure losing your family was difficult, but refusing to open yourself up to caring about someone else isn't the answer, either. Don't you see? Caring for others is part of taking care of yourself, too."

"I don't know," he murmured. "But it still seems wrong to carry on as if nothing had happened."

"No one is asking you to do that," she pointed out. "I wouldn't want you to act as if you hadn't loved your wife and your daughter. Loving them has made you the man you are today. But I think you also need to consider that love is one of God's greatest gifts. By choosing not to open yourself up to love and happiness, you're actually letting Suzanne and Amelia down."

Zack sat down in the driver's seat and gazed at the sunset, as if contemplating her words.

She sat back down, too, enjoying the rest of the sunset while hoping that somehow, someway, Zack would find his way to peace and happiness, putting the past to rest once and for all.

ZACK COULDN'T SAY how long he sat there while Merry's words reverberated through his mind, but it was well after the final golden rays of sunshine disappeared behind the towering trees along the west side of the lake.

He knew that Merry's assessment was right on, but he still wasn't sure how to let go of the past. And he couldn't help wondering if Merry was right about attending church. Maybe he should try to share his burden with God.

He blinked and realized that darkness had fallen. "Sorry about that." He twisted the key in the ignition and the small lights came on in the front and the back, giving off enough illumination that no other boaters would accidently run into them.

Even in a no wake zone, two boats colliding could be trouble. He should have known better than to sit out in the lake, lost in his thoughts.

"It's no problem," Merry said. But when she huddled down in the seat, he knew she was chilled from the light breeze.

"I have a blanket you can use." Zack set the boat on idle while he lifted the seat cushions in along the back to pull out the spare blanket. It didn't smell too musty as he unfolded it and shook it. He flipped the blanket over her and she clutched at the edge, seemingly glad for the warmth.

"We'll be back at the townhouse soon," he promised. They were on the opposite side of the lake and, with the no wake rule, he figured they would be back in fifteen minutes or so.

Merry didn't say much as he steered the boat and he wondered if she was disappointed in him. Not that he could blame her. This was the second time he'd kissed her in two days and he still couldn't seem to get the tangled mess in his head straightened out.

They hadn't eaten any of the leftovers and he knew that was probably his fault, too. He wasn't hungry, but Merry was still recovering from her concussion and her cracked collarbone. She needed to keep up her strength.

"We should eat dinner when we get back," Zack said.

"I'm not hungry," Merry murmured.

Her dejected tone stabbed deep. What was wrong with him? Why couldn't he just relax and take things one step at a time?

Because Merry deserved more, that's why. She deserved a man who was serious about a relationship. She'd admitted she cared about him.

And he cared about her, too. More than he wanted to.

The last thing he wanted to do was to hurt her. After everything she went through with Blake in the past, and what she was going through again, was rough enough. Merry needed some stability in her life. A man who knew exactly what he wanted. A man who'd share her dreams.

Despite what Merry had said, she deserved the man he'd once been, not the man he'd become.

Zack maneuvered the boat around the lake, the light on

the stern of his boat flickering across a few of the *For Sale* signs. The idea of purchasing a property along the Crystal Lake shore wouldn't leave him alone.

As he approached Julie's pier, he slowed considerably and watched as Merry stood along the side of the boat, reaching for the rope to pull them in, looking as comfortable as if she'd often done the same thing.

It occurred to him that they made a great team.

Merry opened the side door of the boat so she could step out, and Ace followed her. When she was safely on the pier she reached for the bag of leftovers and he couldn't help feeling another spurt of guilt. It was his fault they'd gotten all serious, which had made her lose her appetite. "I'll get that," he called.

"It's okay," she said, turning to make her way up the grassy slope toward the house.

The darkness made it difficult to see, but he managed to get the boat into the lift. He took a few minutes to crank the wheel so that the boat was raised out of the water.

He heard Ace growl and glanced up toward the house.

"Ace down," Merry commanded sharply.

Zack frowned and quickly abandoned the boat lift to catch up to Merry.

"Hi, Meredith," a male voice said.

"Hi, Blake. What brings you here?"

Blake? Zack froze, mentally kicking himself for letting Merry walk up to the house alone, and for not bringing his service weapon. He wanted to rush over to Merry's side, but at the same time, remembered the incident with Leonard. He edged closer, staying in the shadows, searching for Blake. His heart stopped in his chest when he realized that Blake was standing just a few feet away from Merry, holding a gun.

Merry fought to remain calm, trying not to do anything that would set off Blake's anger. She'd learned from her past mistakes that disagreeing with Blake was the wrong approach. He would only get angry and more irrational. At the same time, she was deeply afraid that Blake wouldn't hesitate to shoot Zack, especially if Blake considered him a threat. She hoped and prayed Zack would stay back, out of sight.

"Thank you for the note," she said, trying to keep Blake's attention focused on her. She held onto Ace's collar, unwilling to give Blake the chance to shoot the animal. "What brings you to Crystal Lake?" she asked.

"I came to see you, Meredith," Blake answered in a reasonable tone, as if he wasn't holding a gun. "To bring you back home where you belong."

It took every ounce of willpower she possessed not to turn around to find Zack. Her best chance right now was to treat Blake like a friend rather than put him on the defensive. He was dressed in a pair of jeans and a denim shirt, once again wearing the blue baseball cap. In the dim light it wasn't easy to see his bright red hair.

"Is Caro with you?" she asked, trying to stall. She didn't think Blake's sister would go along with his plan, but if she gave Zack enough time, he could circle around to get on the other side of the house to call for help.

"No. But Caroline misses you, Meredith," he said in a chiding tone. "You shouldn't have left without telling us where you were going."

"I'm sorry," she murmured, wishing she knew exactly

how Blake had found her in the first place. "I miss Caro a lot, too. I miss all of you." And in a way she did, because the fun times she'd spent growing up with the Caruthers family were some of her happiest memories.

But the months she'd spent dating Blake were also her saddest and darkest memories. As nice as he sounded right now, she knew full well he was capable of killing her. Especially if he found out she had no intention of going back with him.

"How is David? And Joey?" she asked, hoping she could gain a few minutes by discussing Blake's siblings.

Blake waved the gun as if they weren't important. "There will be plenty of time for you to catch up with the rest of the family later. Right now, you need to come with me."

She tightened her fingers on Ace's collar as fear shimmered along her spine. No matter what he threatened, she couldn't bear the thought of going with him.

Help, me, Lord! Show me the way!

"You'll have to give me a few minutes to pack my things," she said, playing along with him. "If you'll wait here, I'll be right back."

"I don't think so," Blake said in a harsh tone. "Do you think I'm stupid?"

She swallowed hard and tried not to back away from him, even though he was beginning to show the depth of his mental illness. She reminded herself that it wasn't his fault that he had a mental illness. Although it had been Blake's choice not to take his medication, which brought them full circle.

"I didn't say that, Blake. You were always smarter than me in school, remember?"

Blake took a few agitated steps making Ace growl again.

"Easy boy," she whispered.

"Do you have any idea what I've gone through while you've been gone?" Blake asked harshly. "And what I had to go through to find you? And then come out here without getting caught?"

She couldn't sense Zack behind her, which gave her hope that he was on his way to getting help. How long before the sheriff's deputies would get here? She had no idea.

"That was you out in the fishing boat, wasn't it?" she asked. "And that was you I saw looking into my kitchen window, too, wasn't it? Why didn't you say something? Or come inside to talk to me, then?"

"You know why," Blake said, pacing again, back and forth in an agitated way. "Because that man was there. I thought about trying to kill him, but first I had to get away."

Her blood ran cold as Blake voiced her greatest fear. She couldn't bear to think of Zack getting hurt, or worse, because of her.

A wave of helplessness washed over her. What if Blake never got over his obsession with her? What if she ended up running away from him for the rest of her life?

"Is he your boyfriend now?" Blake demanded. "Did you move here because of him?"

"No, Zack isn't my boyfriend," she said. "He's the brother of a friend, that's all. I haven't dated anyone since you, Blake."

Blake twitched and glanced over to his right, as if seeing something that wasn't there. "I know, I know. We have to go. Soon."

Her stomach clenched with fear as she recognized the outward sign of Blake's hallucinations. At times he could seem so rational, so normal, and then suddenly he was talking to people who weren't there.

And if he was losing his grip on reality, there would be no way to reason with him.

"I'll just put the dog inside the house, so he doesn't run away," she said, taking a step sideways to get closer to the house.

"No!" Blake's sharp tone made her jerk her head backward, as if expecting a slap. "We have to go now, don't you see? Everyone is waiting for us."

"We can't take the dog with us, Blake," she said striving to sound reasonable. "I'll just put him inside where he'll be safe."

Blake mumbled something she couldn't hear as he turned and walked several steps away before spinning back around to face her. "Why do you have a dog?"

"He's not my dog," she tried to assure him. "I'm just taking care of him."

"Fine, but hurry up. We have to get out of here."

She wanted nothing more than to get Ace inside the house where he'd be safe, but something on the grass in the area behind where Blake had been standing caught her attention. She frowned, trying to figure out what it was.

A shoe? Why would there be a shoe there? As she stared at the sight, she realized the shoe was attached to a leg.

Dear Lord, was there a person lying on the ground? Had Blake already shot and killed someone?

And if so, who?

13

Zack crept along the farthest edge of the lawn, staying in the shadows of the pine trees as he made his way around to the front of the townhouse.

As soon as he was safely around the corner, he broke into a jog and pulled out his cell phone to dial 911. The ringing on the other end of the line seemed to go on for an exceptionally long time before the dispatcher answered. "Hope County Sheriff's Department. What is the nature of your emergency?"

"I'm at 2414 South Lake Drive and there is a Blake Caruthers here threatening Merry Haines with a gun," he said in a low voice. He stopped short when he realized there was an unfamiliar car parked along the side of the road. In the darkness he could just barely make out the emblem of the sheriff's star on the side. "There may be a deputy already on the scene. There's a squad parked in front of the townhouse."

"We haven't dispatched anyone to that location," the dispatcher said. "What's the license plate number of the squad located there?"

"First I need you to send additional deputies, but no lights and sirens," he ordered. After listening to her send out the call for help, he rattled off the license plate number.

"I've dispatched two squads to the address," the dispatcher informed him. He could hear clicking of computer keys in the background. "The squad on the scene belongs to Deputy Armbruster."

Zack wondered if Armbruster had stumbled across Blake's black Jeep and followed him here. But then where was the Jeep? He didn't see any sign of it. How had Blake gotten there? The guy must have parked the Jeep further down the street and came up on foot.

"I don't see Armbruster, but I'm sure he's close by," Zack said, hoping he was right. Just knowing he wasn't alone already made him feel better. "Please tell those squads to hurry!"

He didn't wait for the dispatcher to respond, but disconnected from the call. He paused, debating between going inside for his weapon and circling around the other side of the townhouse to sneak up on Blake.

Since Blake was armed, Zack figured he needed to even the odds. Even if Armbruster was already behind Caruthers, Zack would prefer to be armed, too. He silently opened the front door and used his key to get inside. Forgoing lights, he felt along the wall until he found the hallway that lead to the two bedrooms. He found his service revolver on the top of his duffel bag, and then went back through the townhouse the same way he came in.

Zack stayed close to the house as he went around to the other side so he could sneak up behind Blake. When he reached the corner of Julie's garden, he abruptly stopped, staring at the ground in horror.

Armbruster was sprawled face down on the grass. And

there was only one explanation. Zack was very much afraid Blake had shot and killed the deputy. They hadn't heard a gunshot while out on the lake though, so either Caruther's weapon had a silencer or he used some other type of weapon on him.

He was thankful he'd gone to get his gun as he planned his next steps, knowing that backup wouldn't arrive for at least five to ten minutes.

Zack listened to Merry's attempt to reason with Caruthers and sent up a quick prayer for her safety.

Then he lowered himself to a crouch, easing into a position where he could see Caruthers. The man was pacing erratically and occasionally talking to himself.

He didn't want to shoot the guy, especially if there was any chance of hitting Merry. But he would shoot if he had no other choice.

Zack hoped Merry would keep her distance, giving him room to maneuver. But just then he caught sight of her stepping closer to Caruthers.

Where was Ace? He couldn't see any sign of the dog, which was odd since he'd heard Ace growling at the guy, earlier. He wished Merry had kept the dog close at hand, just in case. And why on earth did it seem like she was going along with Caruthers?

He wanted to shout at her to stay away, but all he could do was wait and watch for an opportunity to take Caruthers out.

MERRY DIDN'T WANT to walk any closer to Blake, but since he

was waving the gun at her again, didn't have much of a choice. She couldn't tear her gaze from the shoe. She'd stalled as long as possible after putting Ace inside the house, but Blake was getting more and more agitated. She felt bad for Blake having to wrestle with his demons, but she also knew he was partly responsible.

"Where have you been staying?" she asked, hoping that if Zack was nearby, he could find a way to follow them. "At the campsite?"

Blake laughed a horrible sound that grated along her nerves. "I was there at first, but for the past two days I've been staying right next door to you, Meredith."

She tried not to gape at him. "Really? Where?"

"At the house two doors down from you that's for sale," he said in a smug tone. "I jimmied the basement window to get inside. Pretty smart, huh?"

As much as it pained her to admit it, Blake's idea of staying in a vacant house was a stroke of genius. No wonder they hadn't been able to find him. And now she knew how he'd disappeared so quickly the day he'd peered in the kitchen window.

Had he laughed as he watched Zack run around looking for him? The idea made her shiver. They were so lucky that Blake hadn't tried shooting Zack back then.

"Is that where we're going now?" she asked. A brief movement from the corner of the house caught her eye, and she breathed easier knowing that Zack was nearby.

Now she just needed to think of a way to disarm Blake before he started shooting.

But how?

She stopped in her tracks and it took Blake a moment to realize she wasn't coming along. "What are you doing?" he asked.

"Did you hurt someone, Blake?" she asked. "I see someone lying on the ground over there."

Blake didn't so much as glance behind him. "He tried to stop me, but I took care of him. Let's go. Now! Or I'll have no choice but to hurt you."

It was on the tip of her tongue to point out that he had a choice, but she bit back the argument. "I'm a nurse, remember? If that man is hurt I need to go and help him."

From the corner of her eye she noticed Zack edging closer. When he scowled, she belatedly realized she should have been trying to get Blake further away from Zack's hiding place rather than bringing attention to the area.

The moment Blake's attention was diverted, Merry slid her injured arm from the sling and rushed toward him, grabbing his gun hand and pushing it upward towards the sky. As if reading her mind, Zack charged forward at almost the exact same time, hitting Blake in the back of the head.

The sound of a gunshot echoed through the night, but then Blake crumpled to the ground. Zack quickly disarmed him.

"Are you okay?" Zack asked harshly.

"I'm fine," she murmured her ears still ringing from the sharp retort of the gun. She could barely hear Ace barking madly from inside the house.

"Can you find something to tie him up with?" Zack asked, turning Blake onto his stomach and yanking his arms behind his back. Blake groaned and tried to struggle. "See if Armbruster has his handcuffs with him."

Deputy Armbruster! She ran towards the prone figure. She pulled off the handcuffs from his belt and handed them to Zack before going back to kneel beside the deputy to feel for his pulse.

Please be alive, she whispered as she placed her fingers

along the side of his neck. At first she was worried she was feeling her own racing heartbeat, but then realized the reassuring slower beat belonged to the deputy.

"Zack, he's alive!" she called out. "We need an ambulance, stat!"

"Just give me a minute," Zack said. She could hear him phoning for an ambulance. She couldn't see much, but felt along the deputy's arms and legs, searching for some sort of wound.

"Devon? Can you hear me?" She hoped using his first name would get through to him.

Deputy Armbruster began to groan seconds before two additional deputies arrived on the scene.

"Where's Caruthers?" Deputy Thomas asked.

"Zack has him handcuffed. Devon is hurt and I'm afraid to move him."

"The ambulance should be here any minute," Deputy Thomas assured her. "Ian, shine your flashlight over here," he called out to the other deputy.

She couldn't see Deputy Ian Kramer as he was holding the flashlight, but at least now she could do a better job of examining Devon. Her fingers stumbled across a huge knot on the back of his head, and she winced in sympathy knowing he was going to have a concussion or worse.

"I don't see any bullet wounds," she said half under her breath.

Devon groaned again and she decided that maybe they could log roll him onto his back. "Tuck his arm along his side," she told Deputy Thomas. "I'll support his head and his neck as we roll him over."

"You're injured," Zack said, coming over to kneel beside her. "I'll do it."

She'd been ignoring the ache in her broken collarbone,

knowing that Deputy Armbruster was hurt far worse. Besides, it was worth it to get Blake under control.

"I'm alright," she protested, but sat on her heels to let Zack and Jason Thomas roll Devon over onto his back.

"What happened?" Devon asked hoarsely. "Where am I?"

"You're at Julie and Derek's townhouse," she said. "Where do you hurt the most?"

"My head," Devon whispered. "I was following Caruthers, or at least the guy I thought was Caruthers, but I should have called for backup right away. I wanted to be sure he was our guy, first, but I underestimated him."

"It's all over, we have Blake in handcuffs," she assured him. "Do you hear the ambulance? Help is on the way."

Devon Armbruster's eyes slid shut as if the light from Ian Kramer's flashlight was too much. She knew just how he felt. As soon as the paramedics arrived, she gave them a brief summary.

"Hi, Sam," she greeted the young man who was Sheriff Torretti's son. "I'm fairly certain Deputy Armbruster has a concussion, and so far I haven't found any other injuries."

"Good to know," Sam said as he deftly started a peripheral IV. He glanced over at Deputy Thomas. "You better let my dad know about this."

Deputy Thomas nodded. "I know. The sheriff isn't going to be happy at losing another deputy, even temporarily."

Sam grimaced. "That's for sure."

Within moments Sam and his partner had the deputy bundled onto the gurney. As they whisked Devon away, Deputy Thomas and Deputy Kramer went over to take Blake into custody.

"Make them stop yelling at me!" Blake shrilled as they hauled him to his feet. "Make them stop!"

"Who's yelling at you?" Deputy Thomas asked. "What are you talking about?"

"He needs psychiatric care," Merry said as Blake continued to talk nonsense. "You'll need to take him to the hospital."

"I hit him in the back of the head, too, so you might need to rule out a concussion," Zack added. "And here's the gun he was pointing at Merry."

"We'll drop him off at the hospital first, but then we're going to need statements from both of you," Deputy Thomas said. "I know we've been looking for his vehicle, too. Any idea where it might be?"

"He claimed he was staying at the empty house a few doors down that's for sale," Merry informed them. "It could be that he's been hiding the Jeep inside the garage."

"Very clever," Ian Kramer said. "How is it that someone who hears voices screaming at him can manage to be so deviously smart by breaking into an empty house?"

"I don't know," Deputy Thomas acknowledged. "Blake Caruthers, you're under arrest for assaulting a police officer, identity theft, and violating your no contact restraining order."

Merry felt the warmth of Zack's arm around her shoulder and leaned into him as she listened to Deputy Thomas giving Blake his Miranda rights. She didn't bother to point out that since Blake wasn't psychologically stable, reading him his Miranda rights was useless.

"Are you sure you're not hurt?" Zack asked.

"I'm fine. Thank you for not shooting him."

"I couldn't believe you rushed at him like that," Zack said in an incredulous tone. "You nearly took ten years off my life with that stunt. And I wasn't going to shoot him except as a last resort. It's not his fault he's ill."

She sighed. "If only he'd take his meds."

"You can't fix him, Merry."

"I know." She couldn't believe the nightmare was finally over. At least for now. "Do you know how long he'll be in jail this time?" she asked.

"I think we can make a case that he needs a court order to force him to take his meds," Zack said. "He needs help, not jail."

She agreed, although she feared she'd never feel safe knowing Blake was out of jail and able to come and find her.

Loud yelling coming from the front of the house startled her. "What's going on?"

"I don't know," Zack said grimly.

She followed as Zack took off running in the direction that the deputies had taken Blake. When they reached the street, she stopped when she saw Deputy Thomas kneeling beside Blake's body.

"What happened?" Zack asked.

"He started fighting and head-butting us," Deputy Thomas said. "He broke free, and when Ian tackled him, Caruthers hit his head on the ground. Now he's not moving."

Merry rushed forward and felt for a pulse. "We need to start CPR!"

Both deputies worked together to perform cardiopulmonary resuscitation while Zack called for another ambulance. When they got tired, she and Zack took a turn.

They worked continuously until the ambulance got there, and once the paramedics gave him some meds, his pulse returned.

When the ambulance took off with red lights and sirens blaring, she turned to Zack. "We need to get to the hospital."

"I'll drive."

She prayed for Blake's well-being as Zack drove, regretting her earlier negative thoughts. Granted, she didn't want to have the threat of Blake coming after her hanging over her head, but she never wanted him to die, either.

Zack parked as close to the ER as possible, and when they rushed in, she couldn't tell by their serious expressions if the news was good or bad.

"Are they still working on him?" she asked.

Deputy Thomas slowly nodded. "Yeah, he's better, although they're still worried about a potential head injury.

She nodded, knowing firsthand how a concussion felt. "Why do you think he tried to run away?"

"I don't know," Deputy Kramer admitted. "Maybe the voices in his head told him to?"

"Or maybe he tried to run because he'd committed other crimes," Zack pointed out.

Dr. Gabe Allen came into the waiting room, his eyes widening when he recognized Merry. "What are you doing here?" he asked.

She couldn't seem to dredge up a smile. "The man you're working on, Blake Caruthers, was a former friend of mine. How is he?"

Gabe nodded. "He's okay. We've stabilized him. We'll need to keep an eye on him for the next few days but I think he'll be fine."

Despite her fear of Blake, she was glad he hadn't died. She hoped and prayed that this time he'd get the help he needed.

"But hitting his head shouldn't have caused a heart attack. Why do you think caused his heart trouble?" she asked.

Gabe hesitated. "We don't know for sure," he hedged. "We're checking all options."

"Likely drugs, right?" Merry knew by the look on Gabe's face that she'd guessed right. "Cocaine is known to cause heart problems, and I'm pretty sure Blake used drugs in the past."

Gabe shrugged, neither confirming nor denying her statement.

"I'm glad to hear he's okay," Ian said. "At least now I won't have to be accused of purposefully trying to get rid of the guy."

"You were only doing your job," Zack assured him. "He was mentally unstable and armed. We all did our best tonight."

Merry nodded her agreement, knowing they were right. She didn't know how long Blake would be jailed this time, but hopefully long enough that she wouldn't have to look over her shoulder and worry about him coming after her for a long time.

Still, she couldn't help wishing he'd go back on his medication. She missed the young Blake she'd idolized in high school. The one who'd been like a big brother to her.

Please, Lord, please take care of Blake. Bring him peace.

14

Zack blinked at the sunlight pouring into the bedroom and shot bolt upright, afraid he'd overslept. He peered at the clock, relieved to note that it was still early. Merry planned on going to church and he'd promised to go along.

They hadn't gotten home from the police department until late, and then he'd gotten a call from Cole telling him they found Calvin Reynolds dead body at Caruthers' place. It seemed that Reynolds hadn't given up his identity without a struggle. He was secretly glad to know that Blake would spend a long time behind bars once the police had proved he'd murdered Reynolds.

He wasn't sure how Merry had felt about hearing the news that Blake likely killed a man. She'd been unusually quiet last night on the way home.

Still, knowing Merry, she wouldn't take the excuse of fighting with her stalker, doing CPR on him, and being up late in order to give her statement to the police to beg off from singing in the church choir.

Zack quickly showered and changed his clothes, wishing he'd brought something nicer than a simple pair of tan Dockers and a polo shirt. Still, anything was better than jeans.

He ate a quick bowl of instant oatmeal before heading outside on the patio to see if Merry was up. She was just finishing her own breakfast, and when Ace whined at the door, she looked surprised to see him. "Good morning, Zack."

"Good morning." He opened the door to let Ace outside. "Did you manage to get some sleep?"

She grimaced and nodded. "Yes. One minute I was praying for Blake and the next my alarm was going off."

He smiled, thinking it was a good thing that God was watching over her. "I'm ready to leave anytime you are."

"Are you sure? I'd like to be there early if you don't mind."

"I figured as much. You and the rest of the choir have to warm up first, right?"

She smiled and nodded. "Just give me a minute to get my purse."

"Come on, Ace," he called. The dog watered a tree, and then came bounding back to the patio. Zack rubbed Ace behind the ears while he waited for Merry.

"Back inside, Ace," he said, opening the patio door and urging the dog inside.

"Come on in. We'll go out the front door," Merry said.

He stepped inside, making sure to lock the screen door behind him. When he saw Merry dressed in a pretty blue flowered dress, he had to remind himself to breathe.

"You look great," he managed.

"Thank you," she said softly. As inappropriate as it was,

he couldn't help thinking about their kiss as he followed her outside to his truck.

He couldn't think of a single intelligent thing to say as he drove to church, not wanting to remind Merry about the events from last night. He couldn't help wondering how her collarbone was feeling, since she'd insisted on doing CPR while they'd worked on Blake.

"Thanks for coming to church with me," she said, breaking into his thoughts.

"I don't mind," he said, somewhat surprised to realize it was true. When he'd prayed last night for Merry's safety, he realized that maybe she'd been right. God hadn't given up on him after all.

He regretted the fact that he only had one more day off work. He didn't want to leave Merry and return to Madison. But he also didn't think he could give her what she deserved.

Maybe he needed to pray for God's guidance?

"I'll drop you off, and then find a place to park," he said, pulling up to the church.

"Okay, I'll see you after the service." When she climbed out of the truck he realized she was wearing her sling again. No doubt because her collarbone was hurting.

He parked his truck and walked toward the front door, trying to think of a way to convince Merry to go back to the hospital for another X-ray. What if she'd dislocated the fracture? What if she needed surgery?

He stayed outside near a group of church members who'd gathered to chat. Seeing everyone greeting each other reminded him how much he'd once liked being a part of the church community.

"Daddy," a little girl grabbed onto his pants leg, and he glanced down at her in surprise. She was a cute toddler, and when she saw him her tiny face puckered into a frown.

"Hey Kayla, that's the wrong daddy," a woman said, coming over to the rescue. "Sorry about that," she said with a gentle smile. "My husband, Gabe, is wearing the same pants, and Kayla must have gotten a little confused."

"No problem," he said, glad to see that the little girl was smiling again. When a tall man came over to join them, he recognized him as Dr. Allen.

"Hi," Gabe greeted him. "Didn't I just see you last night?"

"Yes, you did. I'm Zack Crain," he introduced himself.

"Oh, you're Julie's brother, aren't you?" Gabe exclaimed with a smile. "Of course, I should have noticed the resemblance. This is my wife, Larissa and our one year old, Kayla."

"Nice to meet you." Zack usually avoided little kids, especially those who reminded him of Amelia, but for some reason, being close to Kayla wasn't too bad. "Your daughter is adorable."

"Thanks," Gabe said.

"Let's hope she likes being a big sister," Larissa said, putting her hand on her stomach.

It wasn't until then that Zack realized Larissa and Gabe were expecting another baby. "Are you hoping for a boy this time?" he asked.

"It doesn't matter one way or the other," Gabe said. "We'll love every child we bring into the world, no matter what."

Zack nodded, and when the church bells rang they all filed inside.

As he sat through the church service, listening to Merry's beautiful voice and the pastor's sermon, he couldn't get Gabe Allen's comment out of his mind.

Why had he thought that having another child would replace Amelia in his heart? Gabe was right, each child deserved to be loved for his or herself. Loving Suz and Amelia didn't mean he couldn't love anyone else.

What an idiot he'd been. All this time he'd held onto his grief and his anger, turning his back on God and the church.

He bowed his head and prayed for forgiveness as Merry began to sing her solo.

And, finally, he embraced an overwhelming sense of peace.

MERRY COULDN'T HELP STARING at Zack during the service, even though she should have been paying attention to Pastor John's message.

Zack looked so handsome dressed in his nice clothes, seated in the pew behind Gabe, Larissa and little Kayla. Merry was surprised that Zack kept smiling at Kayla and told herself not to read too much into his actions.

She couldn't deny she didn't want the weekend to come to an end. Zack would head back to Madison tomorrow, and Julie and Derek would return home the following day.

And she'd be alone, again.

Enough. She really needed to stop feeling sorry for herself, right now. So many others had it far worse. Poor Blake was going to jail for a long time. And Zack was finding his way back to God and the church. How could she be sad about that?

Very simply, she couldn't. So what if she was alone? She'd ask Julie and Derek if she could move in next door and maybe she'd get a dog. A black lab, just like Ace. Or maybe a golden retriever.

She was blessed to have a good job, working with great people. She was also blessed to live in a town that felt like home in a way that Minneapolis never had. And she didn't have to run any more.

Feeling better, she led the choir in the closing hymn and couldn't help but smile when she noticed Zack was singing along.

After the service was over, she expected Zack to be anxious to leave, but found him chatting again with Gabe and Larissa while Kayla climbed up on the pew. She walked over to join them.

"How are you feeling, Merry?" Larissa asked. "I heard you did CPR last night."

Big news traveled fast in a small town. "Yes, but I'm okay."

"Hey, Doc, don't you think Merry should get another X-ray of her collarbone, just to be sure she didn't injure it further?" Zack asked.

Gabe nodded. "Yeah, that wouldn't be a bad idea."

She tried not to roll her eyes. "But my collarbone doesn't hurt that bad," she pointed out.

"But you don't want the bone to heal crooked, either," Zack argued.

"He's right, Merry," Gabe said. "Dr. Katy is on today. She'd sneak you in for a quick X-ray, no problem. You'd be in and out in a matter of minutes."

Since it was three against one, she gave up. "Okay, I'll go in and have another X-ray, but it will only prove that I'm fine."

"Good. We'll go there first, and then we can stop in at Rose's Café for lunch."

"Three days in a row?" she joked. "You're a brave man, Zack Crain."

"I can take the heat," he joked back. "Besides, we didn't eat much for dinner last night and I'm still hungry."

Her smile dimmed a bit as she remembered why they hadn't eaten their leftovers. Not just because of Blake, but because Zack had kissed her.

And she'd kissed him back.

But he couldn't give her what she wanted, a relationship with a future.

"Up!" Kayla demanded, holding her arms out to Zack.

He stared at the little girl in surprise, but then reached down to pick her up, holding her in the crook of his arm.

"You should feel honored," Larissa said. "Kayla is normally afraid of strangers."

Little Kayla rested her head against Zack's shoulder, and Merry couldn't help but think about what a great father he must have been to Amelia.

And what a great husband and father he could be again if he allowed himself to fall in love.

STOPPING off at the hospital for an X-ray didn't take long, although Merry quickly discovered that Devon Armbruster was still a patient up on the same neuro floor she'd been on.

"Do you think we should go up to visit him?" she asked Zack.

"Maybe we should wait for a while. I think his concussion was worse than yours. Besides, Blake might be on the same floor. He's under guard, so you wouldn't be able to visit him."

Merry nodded, thinking about how terrible she'd felt

during the first twenty-four hours of her brief hospital stay. "Your right, I'll have plenty of time to stop in to see him tomorrow or the next day. And I have no plans to visit Blake. I'm hoping at some point he'll forget all about me."

Zack frowned but didn't say anything as they walked back out to his truck.

When he headed toward Main Street, she stopped him with a hand on his arm. "Could we pick up something and eat at home?" she asked. "I'm just not up for all the questions about last night."

"Sure, what would you like? Sub sandwiches? Or a pizza?"

"Let's get a pizza." She could almost smell the tangy sauce and the melted cheese and her stomach rumbled with anticipation. "I haven't had one in ages."

"Sounds good."

Zack pulled up in front of the pizza joint in town and picked up a ready-made pizza. She held it on her lap, trying not to drool as he drove back to the townhouse.

He took the pizza from her hands and carried it inside, holding it high enough that Ace couldn't get to it. "Down boy," he said.

Ace dropped to his feet and she remembered how well the dog had listened to her last night. "Good boy," she said, giving him a good rub.

She let Ace outside and brought out paper plates and napkins so they could enjoy their meal on the patio in front of the lake. Zack put the umbrella up for shade, and then sat down next to her and bowed his head.

"Dear Lord, thank you for this beautiful day and for the food we're about to eat," Zack said. "Please heal Blake Caruthers and bring him the peace he deserves. Please help

Merry and Devon Armbruster heal from their injuries, Amen."

"And please watch over Zack when he returns to work," Merry added. She was touched by the way Zack prayed for Blake, the same way she had last night. "Thank you, Zack."

He reached over and gave her hand a quick squeeze. "Thank you for taking me to church with you. I really enjoyed it."

She wanted to ask more but he released her to take a big bite of his pizza so she helped herself to a piece too. "Mmm, pepperoni, my favorite."

"Mine, too," Zack said between bites.

Being with Zack was wonderful and she wished the day would last forever. When they'd finished the pizza, managing to eat every slice, she sat back in her seat gazing out at the lake as Zack threw the garbage away.

"It's a great day for a boat ride," she said.

"We'll go in a little while, once our stomachs have had a chance to settle," Zack said, sitting beside her.

"Well, maybe you shouldn't have eaten so much," she said.

He grinned. "You managed to eat your fair share."

She laughed softly, knowing he was right. "Zack, I feel bad you didn't get to enjoy a full weekend off work."

He looked surprised. "What do you mean? This was a great weekend for me. You're the one who didn't get to enjoy it very much. I got to swim, ride the boat, play softball and spend time with you."

Her heart stuttered and she took a deep breath, knowing he didn't mean that the way it sounded. "I had a great weekend, too. I'm just sorry about everything that happened with Blake."

"You can't hold yourself responsible for what

happened," he said gently. "Blake was a sick man who did this on his own. I'm glad he's been arrested and that he won't hurt you again."

"Do you really think he killed that other man, Reynolds?"

"Yeah, I do."

"Me too," she confessed. "And as terrible as it sounds, I'm glad he'll either be in prison or in a psych hospital for a long time."

"It's not terrible at all, I feel the same way." Zack paused. "Merry, I'd really like to see you again. After this weekend, I mean."

She tried not to let her shock show on her face. "Really?"

Zack nodded. He turned in his seat so he was facing her. "Today in church, I realized that you were right about everything. God never turned away from me. But after losing Suz and Amelia, I couldn't seem to find my way back to the church and my faith. Until now."

Her heart swelled with hope. "Oh Zack, you have no idea how happy I am to hear you say that."

"Merry, I care about you. But I need to know, do you have feelings for Devon Armbruster?"

This time she couldn't prevent her jaw from dropping open. "What? Why on earth would you think that?"

"The thought of you dating other men makes me feel sick," Zack mumbled. "You seemed so worried about him, I just thought maybe..."

"Of course I was worried about him. Blake almost killed him!" She couldn't believe what Zack had thought and, for a moment, she wasn't sure if she should trust him with her heart.

But then she realized she'd already given Zack her heart. She just hadn't told him that, yet. "I don't have any interest in dating anyone other than you. Don't you know that I've liked you since we first met at Julie and Derek's wedding? I knew you were hurting so I didn't let my true feelings show."

"I thought about you, too, Merry. More than I had any right to. And I'm relieved to know that you're not harboring secret feelings for Deputy Armbruster, and hopefully not for anyone else, either."

"Anyone else?" she echoed. "You act as if I've been dating men all over town."

He scowled. "You might not realize it, but there are a lot of men around here who are secretly dying to go out with you. But please don't. I know I'm asking a lot because I still live in Madison, and it won't be easy to mesh our schedules, but I'm asking you to give me a chance. Give us a chance."

Tears burned her eyes as she struggled to smile. "Zack, I'm not interested in seeing anyone but you."

"Really?" He looked so happy and surprised she couldn't stop herself from baring her soul.

"Zack, I don't want to rush you, and please know that you can take all the time you need. But I'm already in love with you."

His mouth dropped open and she hoped she hadn't said too much too soon. But then suddenly he was standing and drawing her to her feet. "Merry, sweetheart, I don't deserve you," he murmured before lowering his mouth to kiss her.

This time, pulling away wasn't even on the radar screen. She gave herself up to his kiss, trying to show him with actions how much she loved him.

And there was a tiny thrill when he pulled her closer, showing her how much he cared, too.

After what seemed like an eternity, Zack lifted his head, breathing heavily. She snuggled into his embrace, unwilling to let him go.

"Merry, I'm not sure I deserve your love, but I know that you deserve mine," he whispered. "You told me that love was God's greatest gift and I know that's true. I love you, too."

"I know." She lifted her head and gazed up at him. "We have plenty of time, Zack. There's no rush. We'll be together as often as possible and give our love time to nourish and grow."

He smiled and gave her another quick kiss. Ace butted his head between them, making sure that they hadn't forgotten about him.

Maybe one day, she and Zack would have a dog of their own. And a family.

But for now, she was content to wait.

EPILOGUE

Zack stood at the front of the church, tugging on the necktie of his tux, more nervous than he cared to admit. Derek, his best man, put a reassuring hand on his shoulder. "You'll be fine."

"I know." Zack wasn't worried about getting married to Merry. He was concerned that he'd somehow mess up the best thing that had happened to him in a long time. He'd spent every bit of free time he had with her, showing her how to train King, the black lab puppy he'd bought. They'd tried to take things slow, but within a month he'd applied for a job with the Hope County Sheriff's Department, and once he secured the position, he'd moved back home.

And he'd proposed to Merry the night he'd accepted the job.

He loved her more than words could say, and he was ready to have a family with her.

The music swelled and the people packed in the church rose to their feet and turned to watch Merry walk down the aisle. His sister Julie came down first, the gentle swell of her abdomen showing her early pregnancy. Behind his sister came Derek's daughter, Lexi, an old pro at being a flower girl.

And then, finally, the tightness in his chest eased when Merry came forward, escorted by Mr. Abe Caruthers, Blake's father. Zack was thrilled she'd reunited with the Caruthers family and amazingly, none of them held everything that had happened with Blake against her. Especially once they heard he was being tried for murder.

Blake's father kissed Merry on the cheek, and then handed her over to him. Zack took her hand and turned to face the pastor.

He was the luckiest man in the world to be given a second chance at love. And he silently vowed to be the husband and father Merry and their future children deserved.

If you enjoyed this story, please check out the first chapter in the next book in the series, Worth The Wait.

Chapter One - Worth The Wait

"Dr. Katy?" ER nurse Janelle Larson poked her head through the doorway of the patient's room. "The trauma pager just went off. We have two GSWs on their way in."

Katy Reichert glanced up from the wound she was currently suturing on a young man who'd been sliced by a knife in a bar fight. Now they were getting two gunshot wounds? Barely nine o'clock on a Saturday evening and already patients were pouring in. "Thanks, Janelle. I'll be finished here shortly."

"Sounds good. I'll make sure the trauma bays are well stocked." Janelle flashed a quick smile and darted back out of the room.

Katy concentrated on finishing her task, even as her stomach clenched with anxiety. Hope County Hospital wasn't normally so busy, but with spring giving way to summer, it seemed that locals and tourists alike were determined to celebrate the warm weather by drinking too much and getting into fights. She couldn't remember the last time they'd had so many patients, especially at the same time. Although, truthfully, she'd had far worse nights when she'd been practicing at Baltimore General.

She shied away from the painful memories of her past and focused on the issue at hand. Her patient, Danny Truitt, snored loudly, no doubt from the combination of the alcohol he'd consumed prior to the knife fight and the pain medication he'd been given here. She finished up Danny's sutures—fourteen in all—stripped off her gloves, washed her hands, then quickly logged in to the computer to complete her orders.

"All finished?" Merry Crain, another ER nurse, asked as she breezed into the room.

"Yes, but we'll need to monitor him closely until he sobers up. We can't discharge him until he's fully awake."

"I'll get him hooked up to the telemetry and pulse ox," Merry agreed. "That way we'll hear the alarms if his condition changes."

"Good idea. We'll need all hands on deck for the traumas." Katy headed over toward the trauma bay, anxious to hear more about their impending arrivals. She looked around but didn't see her colleague, trauma surgeon Wade Matthews. Where was he? He was the trauma surgeon on call; his pager should have gone off by now, alerting him to the GSWs.

Janelle was standing near the computer, making sure everything was ready to go. Katy stripped off her lab coat and tossed it over one of the chairs along the back counter that housed several computers before crossing over to Janelle.

"What do we know so far?" she asked.

"Not much. One patient has a gunshot wound to the upper chest, and the other has a gunshot wound to the arm," Janelle said. "They should be here any minute."

Katy nodded. "We should put University Hospital in Madison on alert for the GSW to the chest."

"I already made the call," Janelle assured her. "It's protocol to let them know about serious traumas. The Lifeline helicopter is on its way. They've agreed to remain on standby up on the landing pad."

Katy nodded, wishing they'd dispatched the chopper to

the scene. But it was too late now. She took a deep breath and let it out slowly. Seconds later, the double doors leading in from the ambulance bay burst open, and a bevy of people crowded through.

"GSW to the chest, bleeding badly," the paramedic announced. "We've been pumping O neg blood into him like crazy."

Since there was still no sign of Wade Matthews, Katy had no choice but to step up and take control. "Get the level one rapid infuser," she ordered. "Give four units of O neg, and order some fresh frozen plasma as well. I need a set of vitals as soon as possible."

Janelle deftly connected the tubing and began hanging blood products. Another nurse began connecting the patient to the heart monitor.

"Merry, find Dr. Matthews, *stat*!" Katy drew on gloves and a gown over her scrubs, anticipating blood splatters. She lifted the dressing from the patient's upper-left chest. Blood pooled rapidly, indicating a nicked artery and, likely, a severely injured lobe of the lung. She wasn't a surgeon, but if she didn't take immediate action, this man would bleed to death.

"Get me a chest tray and suction," she ordered. "And start a propofol drip to put him under. I need to explore this wound."

Janelle shoved the chest tray on a bedside table located to her right, and Katy forced herself to remain calm as she waited for the nurse to begin the propofol infusion so that her patient wouldn't feel any pain. She sent up a silent prayer for strength as she picked up the scalpel. A bead of sweat trickled down the side of her face when she opened the entry wound so that she could assess the damage.

Somehow, she managed to drown out the cacophony of voices surrounding her to focus on the emergency situation at hand. She needed to find a way to stop the bleeding. Through the opening, she could see the bullet was lodged in the upper lobe of the lung, which wasn't good. But when she continued her search and found a lacerated artery, pumping out blood at an alarming rate, her stomach dropped.

She hadn't repaired an artery this large or removed a significant portion of lung tissue since her residency, but what choice did she have? How else could she stop the bleeding and remove the bullet? Performing surgery wasn't her strong suit, but she knew they needed to buy time in order to stabilize the patient so he could be flown to Madison.

"Hand me a scalpel," she forced herself to say, hoping the tremor in her tone didn't betray her lack of confidence. The only positive note was that the injury was located high enough that she didn't need to split the patient's chest.

With the scalpel in hand, she opened the entrance wound and placed small vascular clamps to stop the bleeding. She'd need to work fast, or the surrounding tissue would die from lack of oxygen. She sutured the artery, silently praying for strength and precision. When the artery was repaired to the best of her ability, she opened the clamps and breathed a sigh of relief when the bleeding was contained.

Feeling calmer now that the most tenuous part was done, she picked up the forceps and began exploring the upper lobe of the lung where the bullet was lodged. She found herself glancing frequently at the overhead monitor, to make sure her patient remained stable. Halfway through the procedure, Wade Matthews finally showed up.

"You're doing fine," he said, as if his absence was no big

deal. She glared at him, seriously annoyed, but this wasn't the time or place to vent her frustration. "I'll take it from here," he assured her.

She stepped back, knowing Wade's surgical skills were far better than hers, although he wasn't a cardiothoracic surgeon either. "The chopper is ready to take him to Madison, so the goal is to stabilize him enough for the flight."

Wade nodded but didn't look up from the wound. A glance up at the heart monitor convinced her that their patient was doing all right, not great, but better than she'd expected. Her gaze dropped to the patient's face, and her stomach squeezed painfully when she realized the guy was far younger than she'd originally thought—which might be why he was still alive, despite the serious injuries to his artery and lung.

For a moment, Steffie's all-too-still features flashed in her mind, reminding her of the young patient she'd failed back in Baltimore.

"Dr. Katy? Should we get more blood?" Janelle asked, breaking into her thoughts.

"Yes, keep the O neg flowing," she said. She stripped off her gloves and turned to look for the second GSW patient. Her gaze landed on DNR game warden Reese Webster sitting on a gurney with a field dressing wrapped around his left bicep. She'd taken care of Reese just a few weeks earlier, after he'd been slashed by a wounded bear, so she shouldn't be surprised to see him again. Apparently his job often put him in the path of danger.

As she walked toward him, he didn't glance at her, his gaze focused solely on the patient with the chest wound. He seemed more concerned about the other guy than his own injury.

Katy put a hand on Reese's forearm, the warmth of his

skin practically scorching her fingers. She dropped her hand, hoping he didn't notice her hasty retreat. "You should probably lie down so I can take a look at your arm."

Reese's mouth tightened, and he shook his head. "Sorry, Dr. Katy, but I'm fine. Marcus Boyle is the one who needs your medical attention, not me."

She looked over her shoulder to see that Wade had finished with the procedure and was placing fresh dressings over the open chest wound.

"Get those units of blood in, stat, so we can get him up to the helipad," he ordered. "Now!"

Hospital staff and paramedics jumped to do his bidding. Janelle pushed the rapid infuser with the blood transfusions going alongside the gurney, while the other staff members quickly wheeled the patient to the elevators leading up to the roof, where the helipad was located. As soon as they left the trauma bay, an eerie silence filled the room.

"Which hospital are they taking him to?" Reese asked.

"University Hospital in Madison," she replied. "Trust me, he has the best chance of surviving his injury there. They have highly qualified cardiothoracic surgeons on staff. What we did here was a temporary patch job."

Reese stared at the closed elevator door for a long moment. "It's my fault he's injured," he said in a low voice.

"I'm sure there's more to that story," she murmured, feeling bad for him. "Now let me take a look at your arm."

Reese sighed and finally stretched out on the gurney. He was still wearing his forest-green uniform, and he was so tall his booted feet dangled off the end of the cart.

"I shot him," he said bluntly.

Katy unwrapped the bloody gauze from Reese's arm, wincing in sympathy when she saw fresh blood oozing down his arm. His uniform sleeve had been hacked off super short, no doubt by the paramedics to provide easy access to the wound. "I'm thinking he shot you first," she said. "You're lucky the bullet went all the way through. This looks to be mostly a flesh wound."

Reese didn't argue or flinch as she probed the wound, making sure there were no foreign bodies left behind. But when she noted a few threads of fabric embedded inside, she grew concerned.

"I need to irrigate this with antibiotic solution, okay? I can't remember from last time you were here if you have any allergies?"

"No allergies," he said tersely.

All three nurses had gone up with the chest wound patient to the helipad, so she stripped off her gloves to get the normal saline, antibiotic solution, and syringes that she needed.

"Why did he shoot you?" she asked as a way to distract herself from the odd awareness she experienced from being so close to him. She'd come to Crystal Lake, Wisconsin, to get away from the memories of her past failures, not to be distracted by a handsome game warden.

"He was poaching and has been for a long time. I'm sure he injured that bear that clawed me three weeks ago. I've been tracking him ever since, and this time, I caught him in the act of shooting a cougar." Reese's tone was hard and flat. "When I confronted him, he fired at me, so I shot back."

"A cougar?" she echoed in horror. While she loved working in the Hope County Hospital ER, she was a city girl at heart. All this talk of bears and cougars living in the woods that flanked the north side of the lake unnerved her. She enjoyed hiking the walking/running path but wouldn't dare venture any farther. "You're joking, right? There really aren't cougars around here."

A wry grin tugged at his mouth, making him even more handsome. As if his dark hair, hazel-green eyes and broad shoulders weren't devastating enough? "Just a few, and don't worry, they tend to stay far away from people. They're feeding on the overpopulation of deer, which is a good thing."

Feeding on Bambi was a good thing? Katy suppressed a shiver. "If you say so," she muttered doubtfully. "Do you want some pain medication?" she asked, changing the subject. "This is going to hurt."

"No pain meds," Reese said firmly. "I need to drive up to Madison to check on how Boyle is doing."

She wanted to roll her eyes at his macho attitude, but she remembered how Reese had declined pain meds the last time he was here too. With a mental shrug, she went to work, extensively irrigating the wound and then turning toward her suture tray.

"Are you sure you don't want something for pain before I stitch this up?" she asked, stalling for time. Maybe if she waited long enough, Wade would return, and he could do the task. After all, he owed her big-time. Not that Reese's wound needed a trauma surgeon, but for some reason, she loathed the idea of sticking needles into Reese.

"I'm sure."

She stared at him for a long minute before taking a deep breath and picking up the curved needle attached to a suture. Once again, she sent up a silent prayer, knowing she needed extra support from her faith. When she pierced the needle through the edge of his wound, she flinched more than he did. She tried to think of Reese like any other patient, but it wasn't easy. Sweat dampened her scalp and rolled down her back as she placed one suture after another, closing the entry wound and then the exit wound.

And when she finally finished, she stepped back and dropped the suture needle on a wave of relief. For a moment, her vision went hazy, and Reese unexpectedly reached out and clasped her arm in a strong, firm grip.

"Are you all right?" he asked with concern.

She forced a smile. "Of course. You're the patient here, not me."

He lifted an eyebrow, and she inwardly sighed, knowing she wasn't fooling him one bit. She stared down at his hand holding her arm, and he slowly released her.

She forced a smile. "Sorry, I guess I'm a little tired. It's been a busy night."

His expression turned serious. "I know. You were really incredible."

She blushed and dropped her gaze, knowing that if he knew the truth about what had happened in Baltimore, he wouldn't think of her as incredible at all. Her heart squeezed in her chest, and she pulled herself together with an effort.

"Okay, you're all set to go, but I want you to take antibiotics twice daily for the next ten days," she said in a stern tone. "And you'll need to make an appointment with your doctor to get the sutures removed."

"I don't have a doctor," he said with a frown. "Can't I just come back here to see you?"

For a moment, she simply looked at him, wondering if she was imagining the flash of interest in his gaze.

Of course she was. She barely knew the man, had only patched him up twice now. What was wrong with her? She wasn't interested in anything remotely resembling a relationship. She needed to get a grip and fast.

"I'm an ER doctor; I don't have clinic appointments," she managed. "But you can establish care with any of the general medicine physicians here. In fact, I'll be happy to give you a list of names."

He shrugged. "No need, I'll just come back when you're working," he said in a casual tone. He nimbly jumped off the gurney, looming over her from his height of six feet three inches. She craned her neck, tilting her face upward, thinking it was ridiculous that the top of her head barely reached his chin.

"I appreciate everything you've done for me," he said in a low tone. "Thank you."

Their gazes crashed and held. For the life of her, she couldn't manage a single coherent thought. Thankfully, the rest of the medical team returned from the helipad. The moment was gone, and she stepped back gratefully. Wade Matthews disappeared down the hallway while Janelle began cleaning up the equipment and restocking supplies in the first trauma bay.

"Dr. Katy?" Merry called, entering the room with a worried frown etched in her forehead. "I heard the heart monitor beeping and found Danny thrashing around in his room. I think his pain meds have worn off, even though he still reeks of alcohol."

"Okay, don't give him any more pain meds yet. I'll be right over," she promised, grateful for the interruption. She crossed over to the counter, drew her lab coat back on and then rummaged for a prescription pad. Her fingers shook a bit as she filled out the antibiotic order for Reese. When she finished, she carried it over to him. "Here, you can get this filled at any pharmacy, and you need to take these until they're gone. I'd recommend taking your first dose tonight."

"Thanks," he said, taking the script and tucking it in his pocket. "See you soon, Katy."

"Sure," she murmured, distracted by his use of her given

name. It took a herculean effort on her part to turn away to head toward Danny's room.

Maybe it was her imagination working overtime, but she could swear she felt Reese's gaze boring into her back as she walked away.

DEAR READER

I hope you're enjoying my Crystal Lake Series. First let me say, that Ace is a real black lab belonging to my brother-in-law's family and I enjoyed dog sitting for him while they were on vacation. Sometimes there is nothing like a pet to help break through the loneliness and that was one of the main reasons I decided to use Ace in my story.

I have another dog, a German Shepherd Duke in my next story, Worth The Wait.

Thanks to those of you who've written such wonderful reviews of my previous stories, Healing Her Heart and A Soldier's Promise. There are six books total in the series and I hope you give them all a try. Please consider signing up for my newsletter at www.laurascottbooks.com. I only send out a newsletter when I have a new release and I offer a free exclusive Crystal Lake Novella to all subscribers! I also love hearing from my readers so drop me a line if you have time.

Yours in Faith,

Laura Scott

Made in the USA
Monee, IL
14 December 2020

53082927R00111